15 Miles From Home

Book 2 in the Perilous Miles Series

P.A. Glaspy

COPYRIGHT 2018

All Rights Reserved

P.A. Glaspy

1st Edition

Published by Glaspy Publishing Inc

Other works by P.A. Glaspy

A Powerless World Series:

Before the Power was Gone

When the Power is Gone

When the Peace is Gone

When the Pain is Gone

Perilous Miles Series:

300 Miles

Sunday, December 20th

Chapter 1

5:00 AM Eastern Standard Time

The White House

President Barton Olstein was awake, though still reclining in the large four-poster bed in the president's suite. He was going over his speech for the press conference coming up that morning — another attempt to assure the American people that the economy was strong, even as the national debt soared to epic proportions. He had marked out comments he felt made him look weak, or as if he wasn't doing everything he could to make the situation better. *I'm only one person,* he thought. *This isn't my fault.* He was finishing up the last of the changes he wanted made when the sky outside lit up like daylight had come all at once. He turned to the display, mesmerized. After a few moments, the light faded outside as the lights went off inside. In less than a minute, Secret Service Agent Walters burst through the door.

"Mr. President, we have to get you to the bunker. Now!"

The president jumped out of bed. "What's going on?"

Agent Walters was grabbing clothes off the settee at the foot of the bed. "We don't know, Sir, but all the power is out."

"In the city?" the president asked.

"As far as we can tell, Sir, everywhere."

"What do you mean everywhere? The entire country? That's impossible!" the president replied, indignantly.

"Sir, we can discuss this further once you are secure. We have to go now. Come with me please." Walters had shoved clothes, shoes, and an overcoat into a duffel bag which he slung over his shoulder. He firmly grabbed the president's arm and started to usher him to the door.

"Wait! My phone!" the president exclaimed, as he tried to free himself from the agent's grasp to get to his cell phone on the antique bedside table.

Agent Walters held firm. "Don't bother, Sir. It doesn't work."

The president looked at him in shock. "How do you know it doesn't work?"

"Because none of them work, Sir — not yours, mine, or anyone else's, so far."

The president stopped dead in his tracks. "Dear God. Do you know what this could mean?"

Walters prodded him on. "Yes, sir, we're pretty sure we do. They'll meet you in the bunker."

When the president got to the ready room in the bunker, his chief of staff, Vanessa Jackson, was already there. She had on a radio headset attached to a large ham radio-style unit. The ground above them shielded the electronics below. When he walked in the door, he heard the tail end of her conversation.

"Yes, Admiral, let us know as soon as you find out something for sure. We'll be waiting for your call." She took the headset off and handed it to the Navy radio operator seated in front of the unit. She turned to the president.

"Well, what is it, Vanessa? Is it ..."

"Sir, we are still getting reports in, but it looks like we have indeed been hit with an EMP. Everything above ground is knocked out, but we can still communicate with any of the silos, as well as our ships not in port here, and our military bases not in the lower forty-eight. Intelligence is telling us there was confirmation of a missile entering our atmosphere, but before we could launch a counter-attack, it detonated. The altitude was high enough to take out the power grid in the entire contiguous United States, as well as southern Canada and northern Mexico. The country is dark, Sir."

The president stood there in shock, then said only one word. "Who?"

Vanessa shook her head. "Nothing positive on that yet. We only got a short glimpse of the missile before it exploded. However, there is speculation it came from—"

Olstein interrupted her, face dark red. "Russia, right? I knew that asshole was just buttering us up, so he could shove a nuke up our—"

"No, sir. The trajectory seems to indicate the Korean Peninsula."

Olstein was spluttering. "B-but we have a base in South Korea! Thirty-five thousand troops! How could they launch a nuclear missile and no one know about it?"

"We're trying to find that out, Sir," she replied. "Apparently, they have acquired stealth technology from someone. In the meantime, we need to declare a state of emergency for the entire country and find as many house members as we can to declare this as an act of war."

"Ha! Good luck with that. They all went home Friday," the president said with a snort.

"I think the Speaker is still here. I've sent a runner over to his residence. He wasn't planning to fly out until Monday." Vanessa was checking some paperwork she had apparently brought with her. She looked pointedly at him. "Some of the joint chiefs may be in town. However, you don't need any of them or their approval to act right now."

Olstein returned her gaze then changed his focus to a pen stand on the desk. "We can't attack anybody until we know who did this, Vanessa. We have to know for sure ... be one hundred percent positive. I mean, none of our bases will be at full capacity. They have no way of calling the troops in. All hell is going to break loose across the country. We'll need to recall all of our troops to maintain law and order here. We won't have the manpower to launch an attack."

Vanessa rolled her eyes. He wasn't looking at her anyway. *Spineless, as always,* she thought. *I can't believe I've stayed here the whole term.* She said aloud, "Sir, those are valid points, but we cannot appear weak in the eyes of the world. You *know* who's responsible! It *has* to be North Korea! If this attack goes unanswered, every piss-ant country over there will be looking to come here and get their licks in as well."

"Exactly! That's why we can't afford to go looking for a fight. We'll need our troops here, protecting us," he replied defensively.

Exasperated, she barked out, "We don't have to look for a fight — we're in one! We've been attacked! Do you think the American people expect you to just sit here and protect your own ass?"

"How dare you talk to me like that! I'm the President of the United States! I'm the Commander in Chief! I decide what our military will do and where they will do it! We are bringing our troops home to protect all the people in our country, not just me or the Capitol! Get me every top military member we can find. I want all of them back here, *now*!" He stormed out of the room to his sleeping quarters.

With a heavy sigh, Vanessa called her executive assistant, David Strain, in. "David, we need to get in touch with every senior military officer we can find in DC. You may have to go door to door, since we have no cell service or landlines."

David had a confused look on his face. "Um, how are we going to get there? Every modern vehicle above ground is incapacitated."

"Damn. I forgot. One sec." She went to the radio operator. "Get me General Everley. Tell him we need at least four Humvees from the hardened storage over here immediately. Also, tell him the president wants all of our deployed troops back ASAP. When he raises hell about bringing our troops home, patch him through to the president. His idea, he can explain it." She turned back to David. "As soon as the Humvees get here, start trying to find the senior staff in town and get them down here. The shit storm up above may be mild compared to what is going to go down when they get here."

Chapter 2

4:00 AM Central Standard Time

After losing another hour of travel time from an accident caused by the slick road conditions and possibly an inattentive driver, Will was happy to see the sign for the Shelby County line. That meant home was about fifteen miles away. He was singing along with the radio, a classic rock station out of Lexington that had a very wide range. He had saved it in his presets long ago because he could listen to it for over a hundred miles, almost all the way to Memphis. Plus, they played good music. It was starting to fade out though. He sang through the static.

Will stopped singing when the sky lit up the upper atmosphere, almost turning the night to day. He slowed down from the fifty miles per hour he had been traveling, due to the worsening conditions of the roads, and was mesmerized by the sight.

"What the hell was that?" Will exclaimed. As his car stopped running and the dash went dark, he said to his vehicle's interior, "What the hell is going on?" The light faded as his SUV shut down. Since he no longer had power steering, he muscled the car to the shoulder. While there weren't a lot of vehicles on the road, the few cars and semis he could see were trying to do the same. With no power, many of the big trucks just slowed to a stop where they were on the flat stretch of interstate. Others were being pushed by the momentum of the weight of their rigs and loads, sliding on the slushy road. One of them passed him slowly, rear end fishtailing, narrowly missing his front quarter panel.

The night was eerily quiet as everything on the road slowed to a stop and went dark. An interstate with vehicles scattered along and in the road takes on the persona of a junk yard, without the associated rust and decay. Will tried the key, though he was pretty sure nothing would happen. He was right. He peered through the windshield, but he couldn't really see anything. The shadow of a tractor trailer just up ahead; maybe a car off to his left. The lack of headlights, coupled with the cloud cover and swirling snow from the winter storm, had cast the area into almost pitch black. As his eyes adjusted to the darkness, he was beginning to make out other things: definitely a car to the left. The driver had gotten out and raised the hood, apparently thinking it was a mechanical problem. Will watched as the portly man looked over at him, then turned slowly to see the rest of the early morning travelers were not moving either. He started toward Will's car, instinctively looking for oncoming traffic before he crossed. Will got out of his own vehicle with his cell phone in hand, put his coat on, and met the man in the road.

"Hey, buddy, your car not running either?" the guy asked. "Did you see that bright light? That was something!"

Will was shaking his head. "Nope, mine's dead, too. And yeah, I saw the flash. Any idea what it was?"

"No idea at all. You reckon it had anything to do with why our cars won't run?" the stranger responded.

"I think it's too much of a coincidence to think that it didn't," Will said. "Were you heading to Memphis, too? I'm Will, by the way. Will Chambers." He reached out to shake the man's hand.

"Dennis Heath. Pleased to meet you," he replied, shaking Will's hand. "Yeah, my mom lives in Cordova. I was going to surprise her and take her to breakfast this morning then go with her to church. I guess I'll miss that."

Will nodded and said, "I was going to surprise my folks as well. They weren't expecting me until later in the week. I should have already been there. That accident threw my schedule off."

Dennis snorted. "Idiot. Who texts while they're driving, in the middle of the night, in a snow storm?"

"Is that what happened?" Will asked.

"Yeah, heard it over the CB radio. The truckers always know." Dennis wrapped his arms across his stomach. "Man, it's cold out here. I better get my jacket," he said, as he started for his car.

Will walked over with him. "Oh, I should text my sister, let her know I'm going to be even later than I thought I would be an hour ago when I texted her that I was going to be late." He chuckled at himself, then pulled his phone out of his back pocket. He hadn't even thought to look at it until then. He pushed the button to wake it up — but it didn't wake up. He pressed the power button on the side; nothing. "Huh, I'm sure I had a full charge. Great time for my phone to croak."

Dennis reached into the console of his car. "Here, use mine. I hope you know the number. I don't know anybody's phone number anymore. It's all saved in my contacts." Dennis tried to open his phone with the same results. "Okay, this is just nuts. I know it was working, because I pulled up the weather on it right before ..." He stopped, looked at both phones, then Will. "Right before that flash. Holy shit! It took out the cars and cell phones? What could do that?"

Will's mind was racing. *Yeah, what could do that? Even the streetlights are off, that's why it's so dark.* Will gasped loudly. *The visions! Everything dark, no light ... this is it. Whatever it is, this is what I've been seeing!*

"Hey, you okay, buddy?" Dennis asked when he heard Will's sharp intake of breath.

8

Will stammered, "Uh, yeah, yeah I'm good. Look, I —" Will was cut off by a strange sound. It was loud and seemed to be heading straight for them. He looked around, trying to find the source. Then, slowly, he looked up. Heading directly toward them was a passenger jet. It looked to be about the size of a 737. It was losing altitude in a drastic descent. Even though it was probably several hundred feet above them, the sheer size made them duck as the plane passed over where they were standing. They turned to watch as it quickly glided to the ground. It exploded upon impact. A huge fireball went up that could be seen for miles.

"Holy shit! Did you see that? That plane just crashed!" Dennis exclaimed.

This is bad. This is real bad. "I gotta get home. So, what are you gonna do, Dennis?" Will asked.

Dennis was zipping his coat up and flipped the hood over his head. He turned to Will as he put it on. "What do you mean?"

Will looked around and replied, "Well, I don't know what this is but I do know it's nothing good. I don't see these cars magically coming back on. Hell, planes are falling out of the sky. I think I'm going to put on my warmest clothes, lined boots, and start walking toward Memphis. We're about ten miles from the exit to my parents' house, then it's another four or five out to their place. I should be able to walk that. I just wish I had some food with me, maybe a couple of bottles of water. I haven't stopped in over a hundred miles. Whatever this is, I need to be with my family. I'm heading out now. You're welcome to walk with me if you want."

Dennis shook his head. "I don't think I can do that. You might have noticed I'm a tad overweight." Dennis rubbed his hand across his extended stomach. "Plus, I only have these loafers with me. I wasn't planning on staying overnight. I just live in Jackson, so Memphis is an easy day trip for me. I better stay here, see if the highway patrol comes through and can give me a jump or get a tow truck out here. But hey, I've got some extra bottles of water you can have. I always bring Mom a case when I come in. She doesn't drink enough water so that's my not-so-subtle hint to her." He reached into the back seat and came back with four bottles which he held out to Will.

Will hesitated. "Dennis, I don't think the state troopers are going to be coming. If our cars don't run, theirs won't either. That flash lit up the whole sky, so it had to be big, meaning this thing is probably pretty widespread. I really think you should try to come with me. It's well below freezing now, and it's not supposed to get much warmer today, at least that's what the forecasters were saying last night before I left. You could die out here with no heat, no food, nothing but water."

"Well, I'm gonna have to take my chances. Like I said, I'm in no shape to walk to my mom's, especially in these shoes," he said, holding up an expensive leather loafer. "But, you should get going. It's going to take you a few hours to get home. Take these bottles, please." He pushed the water bottles into Will's hands.

Will took them with a "thank you" and went to the back of his SUV. He pulled out a backpack he carried for work. It contained towels, guitar picks, extra strings, a couple of clean shirts, a half-dozen protein bars for when he missed eating before the show, and a few half-empty bottles of water. There was also a small penlight he used on stage if he needed to find something during a show so as not to distract the audience. It was nowhere near full, even with all of that in it. He dumped everything out then started putting things back in with the help of the small flashlight. The towels and shirts went first. He consolidated the water into one full bottle, and added the four Dennis had given him, along with all but two of the protein bars, which he stuck in his coat pocket. He opened his duffel bag and pulled out a sweatshirt and long underwear. Taking off his jacket, he put the sweatshirt on over the flannel shirt and t-shirt he was wearing, then put his coat back on. Sitting on the bumper, he pulled off the tennis shoes he had on. Looking around and not seeing anyone else in the area, he slipped off his jeans and put on a pair of thermal underwear bottoms. After putting his jeans back on, he donned wool socks and his thick winter boots, lacing them up over the bottom of his jeans. He tied the strings together on the sneakers and hung them from one of the backpack straps. Dennis watched in amazement.

"Man, were you expecting a blizzard or something? You know they're usually wrong when they say it's gonna snow around here." He looked at the road and the snow covering his feet, still falling pretty heavily. "Course, looks like they got it right this time."

Will had added two pairs of socks to his bag and donned a knit cap and gloves. "I actually live in the Smoky Mountains. I work in Pigeon Forge. We get a good bit of snow up there at times, so I try to keep clothes in here that I might need if I get caught out in a storm. Nothing you could live outside forever in, but enough to get me home if I need it. When I heard them calling for a winter storm, I made sure I had this stuff with me. After what's happened, I'm really glad I did."

"Yeah, I bet you are. Kind of jealous of you now. So, you heading out then?" Dennis had his arms wrapped around himself and was stomping his feet to keep them warm.

"As soon as I grab a couple of things from the console." Will closed the back hatch and went to the front. Using the penlight, he fished out a handful of mints, some gum, a lighter, and a multi-tool. All of that was added to his pack.

He dug around to see if there was anything else he thought he might need. A small notepad with a pen attached was added. A travel-size bottle of hand sanitizer and tissue were the last things he found he thought he could use. He closed the console and reached into the pocket behind the seat. Pulling out a handful of napkins from assorted fast food restaurants, which he stuffed in the top of the bag, he also found a rain poncho wadded up at the bottom of the pocket. "I wondered what happened to that thing. I'll take that, too." He smoothed the poncho out, folded it in half long ways and rolled it up. Then, he tied it to the backpack in the spot a small bedroll would occupy. Taking one more look around the interior, he grabbed his sunglasses and ball cap. Seeing nothing else he thought he might need or be able to use on his trip, he shut the door.

Dennis was visibly shivering now. "Well, I better get back in my car before I freeze to death out here. You be careful, Will. Stay warm. I hope you make it to your parents' place okay." His teeth were chattering as he spoke.

Will looked at the man freezing in front of him and wished he could get Dennis to go with him. Rather than argue further, Will went back to the back of his vehicle, opened the hatch and pulled some things out of his duffel bag. He handed them to Dennis.

"I don't know if I'll get back here and it's just some clothes. Maybe they'll keep you warm until you get some help. Oh, and take two of these protein bars." He pulled the two out he had stuck in his pocket.

Dennis took the items and looked through them. The top to Will's thermal underwear, a couple of t-shirts, some socks, and a sweater were in the pile. Will doubted any of it would fit the man but maybe he could use them somehow. Dennis held them in his left arm and stuck his right out to Will. "Thank you, buddy. I'll put these to good use. I gotta get back in my car now before I turn into an icicle. Be safe, Will."

Will shook his hand. "I'm not going to lock my ride. If there's anything in there you need or can use, or you want to climb in mine instead of yours, feel free. Mine's a bit roomier than yours." They both looked at the compact car.

Dennis grinned and said, "Now that I will take you up on. Good luck. I hope you make it."

Will waved and started down the highway. He turned back, paused, and replied, "I'll make it." With that, he headed out into the darkness.

Dennis waved back. As he opened the hatch to Will's SUV, he smiled and said, "I don't doubt that one bit."

Chapter 3

5:00 AM Central Standard Time

Carly wasn't sure why she woke up until she realized it seemed a bit chilly in the house, and very dark. The display from her digital alarm clock was black. The soft glow from the light under the microwave over the stove, that was always on and she could see somewhat from her bedroom, was not on. *Great, the power is out. Probably some lines down from the winter storm,* she thought. She snuggled deeper under her blankets and tried to go back to sleep. After a few minutes she realized that wasn't going to happen. She reached for her phone on the bedside table to see what time it was and found it dead. *Strange. I thought I had almost a full charge.* She got up, went to the bathroom, then grabbed a throw off the bench at the end of her bed and continued into the kitchen. Nothing was on — no lights, no appliances, nothing at all.

She went into the living room and hit the button to ignite the gas logs. Nothing happened. A couple more clicks resulted in the same lack of spark. A past experience with the electric starter failing had resulted in Carly keeping a long lighter on the mantle. She turned the key valve off, waited a minute, then lit the lighter. No flame up so no ambient gas. She turned the key back to on and held the lighter in the fake logs. They fired up and she soon had a nice warm glow from the fireplace. She stood there for a moment enjoying the warmth from the flame then went to find her phone charger. She stopped, laughed, and said out loud, "What good is that going to do? No power, dummy!" She went back to the living room and sat in front of the fire.

She wondered what time it was and how close Will was to getting there. After a few minutes, warmed by the gas logs, she dozed off again.

7:00 AM Central Standard Time

When she woke the second time, Carly could see light coming through the curtains of the picture window. Looking around, there was still nothing on, but she could at least see since the sun was coming up. She wondered what time it was. Everything she used to tell time — her phone, the microwave and stove, her alarm clock — none of them were on. *My tablet!* She hurried over to her briefcase and pulled her tablet out. Dead. *Great, I forgot to charge that, too.* She pulled out her laptop and was greeted with another dead device. *Okay, this is ridiculous. There's no way all of my batteries are dead on all of my electronics at the same time.* She went to the bedroom and opened her Kindle. A blank screen greeted her.

"What the hell is going on?" She knew no one would answer her, but it released some frustration to say it out loud. She tossed the dead device on the unmade bed and went to the kitchen. *I have to figure out some way to make coffee, like now.* She only had her pod coffeemaker. Standing in the kitchen looking around, she came up with an idea. She got a small strainer out, the kind that will sit in the top of a glass or mug and set it on top of a coffee cup. She tore off a paper towel and laid it inside the strainer. Taking one of the coffee pods, she opened the top with a knife and poured the coffee grounds into the paper towel lined strainer. She stood back and smiled. "Now to get some hot water." She knew the water in the tap was not going to be hot enough, so she looked around the kitchen again. The blinds on the door leading out to the patio were not quite closed, and she spied the gas grill under a couple of inches of snow. "Ha! That's it!" Opening the cabinet, she pulled out a saucepan and filled it with water. *At least the water still works without power.* She took the pan to the door, opened it, and was immediately met with a blast of cold air.

"Good Lord! It's freezing out here!" she announced to the backyard. She hurried to the grill and opened the lid, sending the snow on top cascading to the ground behind it. She turned the gas on and hit the battery-operated electric start button. She was greeted with an instant flame. She set the pot on the grate and rushed back inside. Shivering, she heard a knock, then a key unlocking the front door. She watched as her father came in. He was bundled up like he had been out hunting in the woods.

"Carly? You up? It's Dad!" he called out as he came through the door.

"In here, Dad. Why are you bundled up like that? Did you not let your car warm up before you came over? For that matter, why are you here so early? Is Mom alright? Is your phone working? Because mine isn't. In fact, none of my electronics work. There's something really strange going on."

Joel had pulled off his thermal boots at the door to keep from tracking any slushy residue onto the carpet. He took off his gloves and hat and was removing a scarf from around his neck as he walked to the living room and stood before the gas logs, hands outstretched. He unzipped his coat but kept it on. He seemed to be short of breath, like he'd been exercising. "Slow down, girl. Let your old man catch his breath. It may only be two miles, but that's a heck of a walk for an old guy."

"*Walk?* Why did you walk?" Carly all but shouted.

16

"Because the cars won't start," he stated matter-of-factly. "Have you tried yours?"

She shook her head. "I didn't even think about it. I didn't need to go anywhere, although I would have if the power didn't come back on, since you have a generator. Why won't the cars start?"

"For the same reason nothing else electronic works, I imagine," he replied.

She looked at him incredulously. "But cars aren't electronic, Dad. They run on gas, not electricity … well, mine and yours do anyway. And by the way, do you know why none of the electronics are working? A power outage doesn't cause that."

Smiling sadly, he said, "Cars are full of electrical components, honey. And no, I don't know for sure why nothing electrical is working, but I have a theory …"

He paused, and Carly waited. After a moment, her curiosity got the better of her. "Well? What is it, Dad?"

He lowered his voice conspiratorially. "I think we've been attacked."

"*Attacked?* Oh my god! By who? How? What do we need to do?" Carly was bordering on hysterics now, looking around the room frantically for a hidden enemy that wasn't there.

Joel reached out to take her hand. "Calm down, honey. I don't know anything for sure. All I know is what it looks like, and what it looks like is that someone hit us with an EMP."

Carly looked at her father with a blank expression. "EMP? What is that?"

"It stands for electromagnetic pulse. Basically, if a nuke is set off in the upper atmosphere —"

"A *nuke*? Did you just say a *nuke*? We've been *nuked*? Sweet Jesus! Will there be fallout? Should we tape up the windows and doors? Oh my god, oh my god … the boys!

17

They're with Elliott! We have to go get them, Dad! How are we going to get to them if the cars don't work? Maybe mine will work, or Aaron's. I'm going to go check ..." She was searching the bar for her keys. Joel held his hand up.

"Carly, I need you to calm down. I guarantee you the cars won't run. As far as Aaron and Cameron's safety is concerned, they are probably in a much better position than we are right now. Elliott would give his life for those kids, just like we would. He's also much more prepared for a situation like this than any of us. Are you cooking something outside?" He was looking over her shoulder into the backyard where thick steam was rising from the grill.

"Shit! The water!" She rushed out the door into the cold, grabbed the pot off the grate and turned the gas off. She carried it back inside and set it on the stove. She closed her eyes, took a deep breath, then looked at Joel. "I think I've figured out how to make a cup of coffee. You in, Dad?"

"Yes ma'am, I am. And make it Irish. I think we're going to need it today."

She reached into the cabinet and pulled out a bottle of bourbon. "Unfortunately, I think you might be right."

~~~~~

Over coffee that wasn't half bad, Joel explained to Carly what he knew about EMPs: that they took out pretty much all electronics and electrical equipment plugged in when the pulse hit; that, depending on the size of the device and what altitude it was detonated at, it could take out a large part of the country; and that if it was widespread, it could take a long time to get things back up and running again.

"How long, Dad? Days? Weeks?" Carly asked.

Joel shook his head. "More like months, maybe even years."

18

Carly looked shocked. "No way! Even if the lines were broken from heavy ice, they get the power back up in days at the most."

"This isn't about lines down, honey. This is about transformers fried. This is substations that will have to be replaced. The power companies don't stock enough to replace them all because they're very expensive. Large transformers can take two years to build, two years for just one, and cost millions of dollars. No, if this is affecting a large area, our lives just changed drastically."

"Well, surely the government will get right on it, start getting everything moving to fix what's broken. They have plans for this kind of thing, right?"

"I doubt there's a plan for something like this, honey," he replied. "I don't think they ever thought it could actually happen. Back when I was on the job, we had conferences about things like this, but they were always referred to like some fairy tale story that would never actually occur. Even so, the gist of it was if it *did* happen, we were basically screwed. The country just doesn't stock the equipment or have the resources to fix something like this. We don't know how bad it is or how far it reaches either. So, we need to make some plans now. We need to load you and whatever supplies you have up in the wagon I brought and get you to our place. As you said, we have a generator and a wood-burning fireplace, as well as all of Mom's canned goods and the chickens, so we should be in better shape there than you would be here."

"Um, okay Dad, I guess I would be better off at your place. I'll get dressed and get some things together. You brought a wagon? I didn't know you had one. Where'd you get it?" she asked.

"It's your mother's gardening wagon. She uses it to haul plants, fertilizer, mulch, that kind of thing around the yard.

Do you still have that old wagon we got you when the boys were smaller?"

She smiled then. "Oh my gosh, yes! Funny you should mention it. I just saw it in the garage yesterday, in a pile of stuff I was thinking about getting rid of this week. But will we need that much room? I mean, we can come back later, preferably after it warms up a little, maybe even tomorrow. We don't have to do it all right now, do we?"

"Actually, I think we should load up as much as we can of warm clothes for all of you, food and water, and toiletries. We should have today, maybe tomorrow, but after that, I don't know."

"What do you mean, Dad? What don't you know?"

Joel furrowed his brow. "I don't know what's going to happen, honey. But, whatever it is, I don't think it will be good. Just think about any time there's been a natural disaster. People go crazy, looting and pillaging; there's lawlessness everywhere. It may not be safe to be going down the street with things like food and water. Did you watch the news last night? The grocery stores were crazy over snow and ice predictions."

"I didn't have to see the news. I was there in it. It was insane," she replied. "I got just what I needed to get through the next few days and got out of there."

He nodded. "I just think we should plan to make a few trips today for sure, then play it by ear after that. I wish we had a vehicle that worked. And I wish your brother was home."

Carly jumped up. "Oh my god — Will! I completely forgot! He was on his way home last night! It was going to be a surprise for you and Mom, him coming in early. He texted me about three and said he was running behind because of an accident, but he didn't say where he was. If his car stopped working on the way, he'd have no way to get home."

"What time did he leave there?" Joel asked, voice now full of concern.

Carly replied, "Nine his time, eight ours. He should have been here hours ago. I don't even know what time it is now, do you?"

Joel pushed the bottom of his sleeve up to reveal an old manual wind-up watch on a well-worn leather band. "My dad's old watch made it through. Glad I kept it tuned up. It's coming up on eight o'clock. He should have been here at least three hours ago, even with bad roads and stops on the way."

"Do we have any idea when this happened? Maybe we could figure out how far along the way he was," Carly said.

"Well, I got up at two-something to use the bathroom and everything was still working. I woke up again about four because your mother's cpap machine had cut off and she was snoring. At first, I thought it might be ice on the lines taking something out. I picked up my cell phone and couldn't get mine or your mother's to power on. I knew when nothing was working, like the phones, it was more than just a power outage. I went to the garage and pulled out our old camping equipment, so I could use the Coleman stove and the percolator to make coffee. I got your mother up when it was done and let her know what I thought was going on and that we had some stuff to do. Tried to start my truck, nothing. I pulled the generator out to hook up the electric, but she told me to hold off for now, to conserve gas. So, I got her a fire started in the fireplace, brought some more wood to the back door, then headed over here to check on you. It's pretty slick out there so I had to take my time. It took me about an hour to get here. It will probably take longer to get back pulling the wagons. We better get a move on."

"But what about Will, Dad? Shouldn't we go looking for him?"

Joel shook his head and said, "Will is smart. He would have figured out real fast when all the cars on the road quit that he needed to start walking. Depending on what he was carrying and where he was, it could easily take him this long to get home, even longer if he ran into any trouble."

Carly looked concerned. "Trouble? What kind of trouble? He won't be going through any bad neighborhoods between the interstate and here. It's Bartlett, for Pete's sake."

"Anything can happen, honey. For now, we'll just pray he gets here safe. Now, let's get busy."

10:00 AM Central Standard Time

By the time they got the first run back to Lauri and Joel's, both Carly and her father were panting. They had piled the wagons as high as they dared, and it was indeed a tough walk with the heavy loads on icy streets and sidewalks. They were met with curious looks, even outright stares, from people along the way. More than a few were out with hoods up trying to figure out why their cars wouldn't start. Lauri met them at the door and hugged her daughter. She turned to her husband and said, "Oh, honey, I'm so glad you're alright. I was beginning to worry."

Joel leaned over and pecked his wife on the cheek. "Now, you know better than to worry about me, darlin'. How 'bout you run back in and unlock the garage door? We'll unload the food and stuff in there."

"Of course, dear. I'll meet you over there." Lauri went back in through the house to the garage. She pulled the latch that unlocked the non-working garage door opener. She knocked on the big double door signaling to Joel that it was done. In just a moment, she saw it rolling up. They pulled both wagons in and he pulled the door back down.

"Why'd you shut the door, Dad? We could use the light," Carly asked as she pulled her wagon to a stop.

Joel looked at her and replied, "Two reasons. One, it keeps some of that cold air out. Two, and more important, we don't want everybody out there seeing what we have in here."

"I don't understand," Carly said, with a confused look on her face.

Joel pulled a lantern from the box of camping supplies he had brought out and lit it with a match. As the lantern light filled the area and pushed the darkness back, he said, "If this thing lasts for a while, which I think it will, people are going to start running out of food and water. When they do, they're going to start knocking on doors trying to find someone to help them. It's going to be a problem, since we've always shared our bounty with our neighbors, especially in the summer when the garden is producing full bore." Joel set the lantern on his work bench and continued. "A lot of them know your mother cans vegetables; everybody around here knows we have the chickens. If they see us bringing in even more food, we could be in for some trouble."

"But, they're your neighbors, Dad. You've known most of them for years. They wouldn't do anything bad ... would they?"

"No one knows what they or anyone else would do in this kind of situation because we haven't been in this kind of situation before. I just know that people who are used to three meals a day, snacks whenever they want, and water coming out of the faucet when they turn it on are going to struggle when all of that is gone." He turned to his wife. "Honey, did you fill the tubs with water while I was gone?"

Lauri nodded. "Yes, I washed both tubs out with bleach and they're full. I went out to the shed and grabbed a bunch of those old milk jugs and filled them, too. I don't know how clean they were, but we could at least use that for washing up if we had to."

Carly's confusion was getting worse. "What are you guys talking about? The water still works. Well, mine does."

Lauri gave her daughter a sad smile. "Ours does too, honey … for now. According to your dad, if there's no power anywhere, it won't for long. What we're getting now is probably from holding tanks and water towers. When it's gone, there's no way to fill them back up."

Carly threw her hands up, exasperated. "So, are you two telling me that everything is just going to go away? No electricity, no water, no gas; no electronics, no cars, no stores — it's all just gone, and we have no idea when it will be back?"

Joel shrugged his shoulders. "Yeah, that pretty much sums it up."

"Well, that sucks!" she stated loudly.

Her father sighed. "It will, indeed, suck."

They spent the next thirty minutes unloading and organizing what they had brought in. Over a cup of coffee, they told Lauri about Will. Carly decided to share Will's visions with them. They both listened intently, Joel slowly nodding his head, Lauri with a shocked look on her face. She became very distraught. "Joel, what are we going to do? How will we find him?"

He pulled her into his embrace. "I'm trying to work that out, darlin'. I'll come up with something. Right now, we need to get back to Carly's and get another load. If this is what Will was seeing, I was right about how bad it's going to get. We need to finish up and settle in until he gets here.

It's a bit slick out there so we have to take our time. Are you good here? Do you need anything before I go?"

She shook her head. "No, but I thought of something while you were gone. Did you try the lawn tractor to see if it would run?"

Joel's eyes lit up. "Damn! I didn't even think of it. How did you come up with that?"

"Well, I went out to check on the hens and gather eggs. Their water was frozen, and I needed something to break the ice. I went into the back shed to find something to use and spied it under the tarp. I didn't know for sure if it had any electronics in it or not."

"I don't either, but we're about to find out!" Joel replied excitedly. He hurried out the back door. Carly was right behind him, with Lauri shrugging into a coat bringing up the rear. The chickens came running over in case anyone was bringing them treats. Joel rushed through them, scattering them across the yard, wings flapping, protesting loudly. Joel called out to them over his shoulder, "Not now, biddies! Git!"

He pulled the doors open on the barn-shaped shed. By the time the women got there, he already had the tarp off. He climbed into the seat and looked at both of them. "Cross your fingers, girls." They both held up both hands with crossed fingers and closed their eyes. Joel reached down and turned the key. The motor turned over and the mower came to life. Joel was grinning from ear to ear as Carly and Lauri hugged each other and laughed. Joel pulled out of the shed and drove it around behind where he hitched a twelve-hundred-pound capacity trailer to it. He came back to where the women were standing. "Climb on, honey. We're riding now!"

Carly got into the trailer and waved to her mother. "We'll be back soon, Mom. Keep the coffee hot!"

"I will, honey, and I'll get a pot of soup cooking as well. Be careful." Lauri blew them a kiss and went back into the house.

"Mmmm, Mom's homemade soup. Hurry, Dad!"

Joel laughed and gave the mower a bit more gas.

Chapter 4

10:00 AM Eastern Standard Time

The White House Bunker

The senior officers were livid.

"How are we supposed to respond in kind to this attack if all of our troops are *here*?" General Everley all but shouted. "And why in God's name would we pull the troops we have out of South Korea? We should be sending every available man and woman *to* that area, not pulling them out!"

All of the military members in the room were nodding in agreement and talking animatedly amongst themselves. All of the Joint Chiefs and a few senior officers were in attendance. The cacophony was getting louder by the second. President Olstein stood up and yelled, "Enough! Listen! With no power across the country, all services will soon stop. No gas for heat or cooking, no running water — we are about to be in the middle of the worst situation this country has ever been in, literally the Dark Ages. Can you even begin to imagine what Los Angeles, Chicago, or New York City is going to be like in just a matter of days? We'll need to set up FEMA shelters at all major metropolitan areas, and the supplies at those locations will have to be kept under constant guard. Our deployed troops may be the only ones we can locate at the moment! I've made my decision! And as far as responding in kind — that would mean sending a nuke over there. Is that what you are saying we should do?"

The entire room responded at once. "*Yes!*"

Olstein shook his head. "We cannot bomb that tiny country without affecting the countries around it. What about the innocent people who would be put in harm's way? What about —"

"What about the innocent people here, Mr. President?" interrupted Admiral Stephens. "As you said, in a matter of days this country will be in complete turmoil. Why? Because that little asshole in that little piece of shit country caught us with our pants down! We need to address this attack immediately, or every other little dictatorial asshole in every other communist country is going to be up our sixes all over the world! Every base, every ship, as well as every man and woman in every branch of our military are vulnerable right now."

"Which is why we need to bring them home, where we are all together," Olstein all but whined. "We need to regroup and get our country back on track."

"With FEMA shelters and emergency supplies?" Stephens exclaimed. "We have nowhere near enough rations to feed the entire population at once, much less long-term," Stephens retorted. "What about the millions of people who *don't* live in a major metropolitan area? Do we just turn our backs on them and say, 'It sucks to be you?' And let's be realistic here. If we bring all of our troops home, most of them are going to go AWOL to get back to their families to ride this out and protect them. And I wouldn't blame them. This is the beginning of a very long, very bleak time for our country. It shouldn't start with us running home with our collective tails tucked between our legs. We need a strong response, Sir!"

Olstein was still shaking his head. "I just can't condone putting our troops into combat mode right now; nor have you made a case that would coerce me to change my mind about recalling them. We will need every man, woman, and child we have to rebuild our infrastructure from this disaster. You're right, we don't have enough emergency stores to take care of everyone. We'll need to set up policing teams to fan out into the rural areas and commandeer resources. Our farming communities will need to donate food and food sources like livestock. We need to take over food processing plants and warehouses; places like Costco, grocery stores, any place that might have large stockpiles of food and water. Plus, there are quite a few of those doomsday prepper types out there who have years' worth of food hoarded up. Well, the day they've been waiting for is here. They'll need to donate most of their stores for the greater good." He turned to his chief of staff. "Vanessa, do we still have access to those records on the purchase history of specific individuals? The ones we flagged because they bought large quantities of bulk food, ammunition, that kind of thing?"

She looked up from the notes she had been taking. "Yes, sir, we had backups stored down here. You should know that was a complete breach of privacy against those individuals, Mr. President. We had no reason to gather and keep that data. They posed no threat to national security, had no ties to terrorist organizations ..."

"And yet, we now find ourselves in a situation where that information is invaluable," he replied smugly. "The needs of the many outweigh the needs of the few. We must all work together to get through this. Some will have to make major sacrifices."

"I don't think they're going to see it that way, Sir," she said. "I'm pretty sure they're going to look at it from the standpoint of 'we prepared for something like this; you didn't. Now, you want us to feed you, to take away from our families? Yeah, no.' Just my opinion." There were murmurs of agreement around the room.

"Which brings me right back to needing our troops back here. They'll go out and gather the extra resources we'll need in the coming weeks and months. Under the National Defense Resources Preparedness Executive Order, we can gather pretty much anything we think we need to sustain our government and military in this time of crisis, from anywhere we find it."

General Everley spoke up. "You mean take, right? You want us to order our people to take the possessions of other Americans, who foresaw an event like this as a possibility, and spent their hard-earned income to buy supplies to take care of their families during a disaster? How is that right?"

"It isn't right that those people should selfishly keep those supplies for themselves when others around them are starving. I won't sit by and watch that happen," Olstein replied petulantly.

Everley shook his head. "Even if I could get mine to agree to that — which is highly unlikely — what about the ammunition you referenced? These citizens will probably be heavily armed and in no way agreeable to *donating* a damn thing. So now, our troops are in as much, if not more, danger at home than abroad. Then what? You're going to order our troops to fire on American citizens, in their own homes, defending their families and property?"

Olstein smiled. "I already thought of that. The first thing we're doing is declaring martial law and repealing the Second Amendment."

The room exploded into chaos. All in attendance were in an uproar except the president. He sat there calmly, waiting for the generals and admirals to get it out of their system. He gave them a minute, then stood and yelled, "Quiet! One at a time!"

The Speaker of the House, Phil Roman, who had been sitting silently up to that point, spoke first. "Mr. President, you can't do that. You don't have the authority. It takes Congress to do something like that, and we can't contact most of the members. And even if we could, they would never do it. They'd all be voted out in the next election."

"There won't be another election for a long time, Phil," Olstein said. "We're going to have a lot more to worry about than elections. We're going to have millions of sick, starving people on our hands. We have to figure out a way to help as many as we can. This plan is the way."

"Sir, your term is all but over," Roman replied. "You have thirty days until the new president, David Tanner, is sworn in. All of these decisions you are making, these edicts you are handing out, are all but invalid at this point. You're on your way out of the White House. Is this how you want to be remembered?"

"Oh, no, I'm not going anywhere. We can't have a changing of the guard, so to speak, in the middle of a crisis like this. I'll see it through to the end, whenever that may be. I'm thinking it will be years before we can get everything back on track. We'll talk about it then. For now, I want our troops home ASAP, and their first order of business will be to disarm the populace and start gathering resources. That's an order from your Commander in Chief. Get busy, gentlemen."

As the president stood to leave, flanked by his Secret Service team, the occupants of the ready room were hurling threats and expletives in his direction. He smiled as he walked out the door.

Rage all you want. There's nothing you can do about it. I wasn't ready to leave. I still have things to do, a legacy to fulfill. This catastrophe is like an early Christmas present to me. I may have to find a way to thank that little prick in North Korea for making it all happen.

~~~~~

31

In the grand ballroom of the Ryongsong palace in Pyongyang, the celebration was still underway. For the past four hours, the top military and party leaders had indulged in food and drink, relishing the victory won with one properly placed nuclear explosion. There were television screens mounted around the enormous room broadcasting news from all over the world about the attack on the United States. Satellite images showed the area completely dark, with lights beginning in the northern half of Canada, and the southern part of Mexico. One could almost picture the range of the nuke by the image from above.

The Chairman was being congratulated by a group of partygoers. One of them queried, "Have you announced to the world that the attack came from us, Excellency?"

Another man in the group responded. "He doesn't have to. They had a glimpse of the missile before it detonated. They saw the trajectory. They know it came from us."

Just as the Chairman was about to reply, an aide came up and touched his arm. The Chairman turned to the aide. "Yes? What is it? You can see we are talking here."

The aide bowed. "Apologies, Your Excellency. There is an urgent call for you. It is waiting in your office."

"From whom? Who would be calling at this time of night?" he replied indignantly.

The aide leaned in to whisper, "The President of the United Nations. He said he must speak with you immediately."

The Chairman dismissed the aide with a wave of his hand and turned back to his guests. "His urgency is not mine. Tell him I'll call him back in the morning."

Chapter 5

6:00 AM Central Standard Time

It had been a little over an hour since Will left his car on foot, but he hadn't gotten as far as he would have liked by then. He received many curious glances from people sitting inside their cars, but the ones who slowed him down were those who got out to ask him questions.

"Hey man, where you headed?"

"Excuse me, sir, do you know what's happening?"

"Hey, buddy, you got any water on ya?"

Being an entertainer, it was ingrained in him to be polite and speak to people who spoke to him. He stopped each time he was addressed, but only for a moment. He had ten miles to travel on roads that were rapidly icing over since the traffic had come to a halt.

"Headed home, hopefully. Take care now."

"No, ma'am, I don't, sorry. Good luck to you."

"I'm sorry, I can't spare any water. I'm trying to get home. I've got about a ten-mile walk. I hope you find some."

However, the man who had asked about the water was not so easily dissuaded. Belligerently, he replied, "Well, I'd kinda like to get home, too, fella. Don't you think you should help a brotha out? Where'd you get yours anyway?"

Will had tried to continue walking, but the man's tone made him stop and turn around. He looked the rude man in the face and said calmly, "I had it with me, *fella*. I've been driving since last night. I always have water with me when I travel. I just want to get home to my family. Do you have a problem with that?"

"Well, I'd like to get home to my family, too! I've got a lot further than ten miles to go. I live in Midtown. How am I supposed to get there with no food or water, much less any warm clothes like you have?" The man was raising his voice louder and louder, getting closer to Will with each word he spoke.

Will knew enough about cornered animals to know the man was scared: scared of the unknown, that being what had happened; scared of not getting home to his family; and probably scared of dying here on the side of the road because he didn't have what he needed to head out on foot when it was apparent no help was coming in the foreseeable future. Will also knew there was nothing he could do to help the guy. He'd be lucky if he made it home himself. He decided to take a different tack and try to help him by offering suggestions.

"Man, I wish I could help you, I really do, but I probably don't have what I need to make it either. I wasn't planning to hike the last few miles, you know? But I think we're only a mile or two from the next exit. If you can get there, you can probably buy some water, some food, at least enough to get you home. Maybe this doesn't go all the way to Midtown. I don't know. I don't even know if I'm just being stupid walking in this freezing cold ice rain because the lights are actually on a mile from here. I just can't sit and wait. Maybe you shouldn't either. Just start walking. If you get too cold, see if someone will let you rest and warm up a little in their car. I'm sorry, but I really have to get moving. Good luck to you."

With that, Will turned resolutely and headed down the road. He didn't know if his even, unexcited tone had helped calm the man down or not, but he called after Will, "Yeah, I might just do that. Uh, good luck to you, too."

Will smiled and continued on his way.

The sun coming up behind him was lighting the sky above and the landscape in front of him. That part of the state is very flat, so you can see a good distance. All Will saw were cars and trucks, buses and semis, none of which were moving, on a road that the snow was covering over quickly now that the warmth from travelers' exhausts was no longer on it. He did see some people out on the road not too far ahead milling about their vehicles. *Great, more delays.* He thought briefly about trying to find a way to skirt the area, maybe going off the road into the tree line, but if he could see them they could see him and heading off the road would only delay him further. And he could tell some of them already had. Will sighed and continued on.

The first people he encountered were a young man with a very pregnant young lady beside him. They approached him quickly.

"Excuse me, mister. Where did you come from? Do you know what's going on?" the young man asked.

Will stopped. "Hi. I came from about a couple of miles back. And no, I don't know what's going on. I'm sorry."

"Well, where are you headed? You got somewhere to go, somewhere warm to wait this out? My name's Spencer, by the way; this is my girl, Jessie. We're from West Virginia. We were heading to my mom and dad's for Christmas — they live in Little Rock. All I know is Jessie can't stay out here in this cold. I don't know what to do."

Will looked at the young couple compassionately. He noticed they both wore Converse sneakers; her coat would not come anywhere near zipping over her extended abdomen. He wore a black hoodie with a denim jacket over it. They had on t-shirts and jeans, and both of their jeans had rips and holes, which he knew was the style for young people nowadays but would be less than ideal for staying warm. He also knew that if the visions were indeed happening, this little family probably would not make it.

He searched for something encouraging, maybe helpful to say. Nothing came to him.

"Guys, I wish I could help you, but I don't know what I could do; and I really have to keep moving. I'm heading to my parents' place as well, but it's still quite a few miles away; and neither of you are dressed for a walk like that; plus, I'm pretty sure Jessie couldn't make it. Right now, your best bet is probably to stay put and see if help shows up. If it doesn't, you're maybe a couple of miles from the next exit. You might be able to walk that, Spencer. If you guys have more clothes, you should put them on. Definitely some warmer shoes if you have them, and hats. It's supposed to stay below freezing today, so you should probably snuggle up in the back seat of your car. I'm really sorry but I have to go. Stay warm and good luck."

Will shifted his backpack back up onto his shoulders and started off. He didn't look back at them, even when he heard Jessie say, "Well, thanks ... I guess. See ya."

He waved over his shoulder and kept walking. He felt like a heel, but there was nothing to be done about it. He couldn't be responsible for anyone else. He needed to get home, and he had to do that as quickly as possible. He decided to start ignoring people who spoke to him. He couldn't help any of them. *Best to be rude and just keep walking.* It would definitely get him home sooner ... or so he hoped.

His new approach served him well for a little while. He got some rude comments — "thanks for nothin', asshole" — and rude gestures, but he didn't slow down; that is, until he ran into a guy standing beside a minivan full of kids. The man stepped out in front of him, so Will had no choice but to stop.

"Look, I need some help for my kids," he stated, as he motioned toward the minivan.

Will looked where the man had indicated and saw four small children peering back at him. They seemed to be close in age, probably between two and six. He then turned to the man standing in his path and replied, "Buddy, I'm sorry, but I can't help you." Will tried to step around him. The guy stepped back into Will's path.

"I don't think you understand. We've been sitting here for hours. No cops, no wreckers, nothing has come through. They're freezing! We need help!"

Will replied, exasperated, "What exactly do you think I can do? I don't have a wrecker, I'm not a cop … like I said, I can't help you. I'm just trying to get home."

The man's eyes lit up. "How far is that? Maybe we could go with you. We were heading to Oklahoma for the week to spend Christmas with my wife's family. We can't get there, and we can't make it back home. We live in Jackson. We were going to stop for an early breakfast right before everything died. My kids are hungry, thirsty …"

"Um, not to sound like an ass, but don't you have any snacks with you?" Will asked. "You were going all the way to Oklahoma with four little kids and no snacks? Or those juice boxes?"

The man's head drooped a bit. "We forgot them at home. We were going to run to the store after we ate and grab some stuff."

Will closed his eyes for a moment, then said, "I think you're about a mile from the next exit. If you can walk down there, you might be able to buy some stuff for your kids. I don't have anything, sorry."

"Wait, what are you doing for food? Surely you have something you can give me for them."

Will shook his head. "No, I don't. I ate a few hours ago and had every intention of having breakfast with my sister and parents this morning. I didn't plan for a hike." He felt the little white lie was justified since he only had four of the protein bars in his bag. If he gave them two, he might be hindering his own chance of getting home. *Every man for himself now, dammit.*

"I don't think I can leave my kids to walk a mile to maybe find some food. Their mom isn't feeling well."

Will glanced into the passenger seat and saw a woman slumped against the door with her coat over her like a blanket, eyes closed, shivering. "What's wrong with her?" he asked.

The man looked at her and back at Will. "She gets bad headaches, especially if she's stressed out. Needless to say, she's kind of stressed out right now. Could you go find a store and bring us something back? I don't carry a lot of cash, but I can give you like ten bucks. Maybe they'd have donuts, maybe some milk. You could get yourself something, too. You know, for services rendered."

Will shook his head again. "Man, I'm sorry, but I can't. I have to keep going. You should try to make it though. Good luck."

With that, Will stepped purposefully around the man and continued down the road. He felt bad for the guy and his family. But he had his own family to think of. *Pretty sure there's going to be a whole lot of selfish people out there now,* he thought. *Might as well get in on it early.*

The next exit was indeed about a mile from the interaction with the guy with the van full of kids. Will decided to get off the interstate and see if he could get some supplies for himself. As he walked up to the gas station, he saw people milling around outside. When they saw him, a few of them hurried over to him. The man who reached him first went straight to the point.

"Hey, man, can you spare five dollars? I don't have any cash on me and the manager will only sell for cash since the cards won't work."

Immediately wishing he had thought to stash his cash in small quantities throughout his clothing and bag, Will shook his head. "I'm sorry, I can't help you. I just need to use the restroom."

A woman who had come up as well snorted. "Ha! Good luck with that. The manager won't let you in unless you show him cash through the door."

Will moved through the small crowd. "Maybe I can offer something else in trade then. Y'all take care now."

"Wait! What have you got to trade? Can you get us some water, too?" the first guy asked. "I'll give you my name, address, cell phone number, email address, whatever you want. I'll pay you back as soon as everything comes back on."

"I can write you a check," the woman added. "It's good, I swear. I never carry cash anymore."

Will took in the scene: at least twenty people standing around in the cold waiting for someone to help them. *And I'm pretty sure no help is coming.* He replied, "Let me see what I can do. In the meantime, that faucet over there is a no-freeze hydrant. You should be able to get water out of it to drink if you have something to catch it in." He pointed to a faucet sticking up out of the ground by the air machine.

The woman wrinkled her nose at it. "Is it safe? I only drink water out of bottles or indoor faucets or fountains. Lord only knows what might have been crawling on that out here."

Will smiled at her. "Yes, ma'am, it's perfectly safe. It's the same water that goes to the water fountain by the bathroom. If you're worried about a bug having been on it, you can let it run for a few seconds first. If you have any empty cans or water bottles in your car, I'd grab all of them and fill them. I think I'd rather have water a bug walked through than die of thirst. It might be a while before things come back on. "

She looked at him questioningly. "What do you mean? It's a power outage. A strange one, since my car quit, and my phone doesn't work, but I'm sure they'll get that all sorted out and have everything back up in no time. I don't think we need to get all paranoid here."

Will set his mouth to a grim line. "I sure hope you're right, ma'am. Excuse me, I really need to use the restroom."

Will continued on to the gas station's storefront. The manager was indeed standing there, arms crossed, behind a sign taped to the door that read, "Machine down. Cash only. No checks. NO EXCEPTIONS." Will reached for his wrist and took off his watch. It was a Bulova Precisionist that was worth over six hundred dollars. He held it up to the door. The manager peered through the glass at the watch, gave a curt nod, and unlocked the door. At the sound of the deadbolt turning, the people milling around rushed to the door. Will squeezed in and the manager quickly locked it back. Those outside started banging on the door and the glass front. The manager ignored them and turned to Will.

"Nice watch. What are you looking to trade for it?"

Will looked to the throng outside and walked away from the door. "I actually have cash. I just didn't want anyone else to know. I need to use the restroom, then I'd like to look around a bit, if that's okay."

"How much cash?" the man asked. "Prices are going up as we speak."

Will headed toward the restroom. "Enough. Be right back."

Once in the restroom, he locked the door and pulled the wad of cash out of his backpack. He had a thousand dollars in twenties and tens. He laid it out on the sink and began dividing it into one hundred-dollar piles. He took each pile and stuck it in a different spot. He pulled out the extra socks he had and rolled some up in those. He stuck a pile in

40

each boot, one in the inside pocket of his coat, both front pants pockets got a stack, he put four in various sections of his backpack, and the last he stuck in his wallet, where it was expected to be. He used the facilities, then washed his hands and face in, thankfully, still warm water. He put his coat back on, grabbed his bag, and unlocked the door. He used the water fountain outside the restroom to fill the water bottle he had used so far. After it was full, he walked into the store.

The people outside had moved back away from the building and were shooting daggers at the manager. He ignored them, standing with his arms still crossed watching Will. Will walked the aisles looking for foods that were high in calorie count which would create energy, resulting in warmth. He took two full boxes of peanut butter crackers from a shelf; one cheese, one plain. All the protein bars he could find was his next choice. He grabbed all the beef sticks and beef jerky on the display. He took all of it to the register, grabbing some travel-size hand sanitizers on the way. The manager looked at him wide-eyed.

"You're buying all that? I told you the prices were going up. You heard that right? Everything is double whatever the price is on it."

Will eyed him suspiciously. "Really? Is that an edict from the corporate office?"

"Price is subject to change depending on the circumstances," he replied smugly.

"Whatever. Total that up and add two cases of that water by the door."

The man looked concerned. "Well, um, my register isn't working. It's gonna take a while to add all this up manually."

Will replied, "Fine. I'll give you a hundred dollars for it. Cash."

"No! That's not enough, not for double," the cashier complained.

"Look, buddy … I'm giving most of this to those people out there. If they get some food and water, they'll stop beating on your doors and windows and may even move along. So, be a decent guy and let me do this. It will save you a headache for now."

Will could see the man was trying to add up the price of the food in his head, but without his cash register or a calculator he wasn't going to get there. Finally, he said, "I'll take one hundred fifty. Final offer."

"Deal." Will pulled his wallet out and handed the clerk the cash from it, then reached inside his coat and pulled out the rest. "There's one sixty. Keep the change. Bag this stuff up for me."

Will pulled out a few of the food items and the sanitizers and put them in his backpack. The rest was placed in plastic bags by the clerk. Will took the bags and headed for the door. He stopped, turned back, and said, "Try not to be such a douche. This isn't your every day, run-of-the-mill power outage. You might want to consider that what you do now — how you treat people — could be how you get treated later. Just something to think about. You have a good day." With that, he walked on to the exit. On the way, he passed a display of maps. He grabbed one for Memphis, stuffed it in his backpack, and continued on. He didn't ask about buying it. He figured he'd paid enough.

At the door, the people outside saw that he was carrying bags and rushed to the door. He set the bags on top of the stack of water cases and spoke loudly. "I am willing to share this with you all, but you have to act civilized. No pushing, no snatching, no bullying. Back up and let me out."

The guy who had first approached him in the parking lot was standing by the door. He turned to the crowd and yelled, "You heard the man! Back up!"

The group backed up a few steps and watched with anticipation as Will was let out by the manager, who quickly locked the door behind him. Will set the food and water on the ground, pulling two of the water bottles out and adding them to his pack, too. He pointed to the man who helped move the crowd back.

"What's your name, fella?" he asked.

"Brandon. Brandon Callaway. Yours?"

"Will Chambers," he replied with a smile. "Look, Brandon, I really need to be on my way, so I'm going to put you in charge of doling this stuff out. I'd go with two bottles of water and two food items per person. There should be enough here for that. Then, I'd suggest everybody get some place warm. I have a feeling it's going to be a long, cold day."

"You've got it. And Will?"

"Yeah?"

"Thanks, man. You're a good guy," Brandon said, extending his hand to Will.

Will shook his hand, gave him a nod, and said, "I try to do what I can when I can. Good luck, Brandon."

"You, too, Will. Stay warm."

Will zipped his coat up, stuck his hands in his pockets, and started back toward the interstate. Under his breath he mumbled, "Again, probably not gonna happen."

Chapter 6

11:00 AM Central Standard Time

The lawn tractor slid on the icy road, but under motorized movement they made much better time. With the large trailer, they were going to be able to load a lot more supplies at once. They saw people still out in their driveways on the way back, even though it was still sleeting and snowing, with hoods up trying to start their cars. They received quite a few more curious looks, but no one approached them as they made their way back to Carly's house. On the ride over, Joel suggested they pull into the garage to stay out of sight of the neighbors, as they had done at his house. Unfortunately, Stan Wheeler, who lived across the street, was outside trying to figure out why his truck wouldn't turn over. When he heard the motor of the mower, which was quite noticeable with the lack of any other noises, he walked down to the street and watched them pull up. He came over as soon as they got in the driveway.

"Morning, Carly, Mr. Chambers. I see you've found alternate transportation."

"Oh, hey, Stan. Yeah, whatever is going on with the cars didn't stop the riding mower. Score one for lawn care." Carly was climbing out of the trailer to unlock the front door, so she could get in and disengage the garage door opener. Her attempt to be dismissive went unnoticed.

"So, you guys got any idea what's going on? I can't get anything electronic to work to see if there's any news reports. The whole thing is kind of bizarre, isn't it?" he queried.

Joel motioned for Carly to go on as he replied, "No, we don't know much either. We're just getting Carly and her boys set up at our place. We have a wood-burning fireplace and camping equipment. We're better equipped for a situation like this. It's too cold out here to not have heat."

Stan cocked his head to the side with a questioning tone. "My gas logs are still working. Aren't yours, Carly?" He raised his voice at the end to get Carly's attention. She stopped after she unlocked the door.

Sighing, she turned around to face Stan. "Yes, for now. I just feel safer with my parents at their house. This is not your everyday 'the lines are down' thing, you know? I mean, is the gas still going to work after a while? How far does this reach? Have you heard any sirens or cars at all? At least there Dad has a gen —"

"A generation of experience that may help somehow. We really need to get busy. It was good to see you again, Stan. Stay warm now." Joel took the key out of the ignition, walked up the drive, and opened the door, ushering Carly inside. The gas logs were indeed still going, and the living room was warm, at least. Joel closed the door and peeked out the front window to see if Stan had left. He watched as Stan slowly turned toward his house, turned back to look at the mower, then headed inside. He seemed to be walking with a purpose. Joel looked at Carly.

"Does Stan have a riding mower?"

"I think everybody on the street does but me. Not that they all need one. The yards are tiny. I pay Wayne Hollis to cut mine. Why?"

Joel chuckled. "I think we might have given him an idea for another way to travel. By the way, honey, I cut you off before you could tell him about the generator. We don't want to spread that around."

"Oh, okay, sorry. I didn't know it was a secret. I mean, it's not exactly quiet, right? People who live around you are going to hear it running."

Her dad replied, "No, it isn't quiet, but we'll have enough people hearing it on our street. No reason to add your neighbors to that mix. Now, let's see what else we can take back to the house. Since we have the trailer now, we can haul some heavier stuff. What do you have in the pantry?"

Carly shrugged her shoulders. "Not much. I was planning a big grocery shopping trip yesterday. Memphis Snowmageddon screwed that up. A couple of cans of tuna and soup, half a loaf of bread, PB & J, some cheese, and most of a twelve pack of beer." She opened the freezer side of the refrigerator. "What about fridge and freezer stuff? I've got some pizza rolls, toaster pastries, a few frozen entrees ... oh, and a sweet rolling ice chest we can put it in!" She opened the door to the refrigerator and peered into the darkness. "I also have a drawer full of condiment packs. Think we'll need those?"

"Why do you have a drawer full of condiment packs?" Joel asked.

Carly replied, "We eat out too much, apparently."

Joel nodded. "So it would seem. Go ahead and pack it in there, plus any ice you have in the ice maker. Maybe your mother can figure out how to cook microwave food without a microwave." He looked around the kitchen. "Any bottled water?"

"Part of a case, plus I have some small juices and sodas."

"Okay, put all that in your cooler if it will fit. I guess you can put all those cup things you use for coffee in a bag, since you figured out how to use them," he said. "Sugar and creamer, tea bags, hot chocolate, any of that stuff. If there's no more food than that, we should be able to get some more of yours and the boys winter clothes and finish it with this trip."

"Dad, I still don't understand why we're taking all this stuff to your house, and so fast. Couldn't we wait a couple of days? It's supposed to warm up. The house isn't going anywhere."

With an earnest look, he replied, "No, but the things inside it might."

"Huh?" she responded, clearly confused again.

Joel took her by the hand and led her to the dining room table. "Let's sit down for a minute, honey. I'll try to explain it to you."

They sat at the table and Joel looked into his daughter's eyes. "Carly, think about any time there's been a natural disaster. What did you see on the news?"

Carly thought for a minute. "What kind of disaster? Flood? Tornado?"

"Any kind. What happens to the businesses in the area?"

"They get looted. People take electronics, clothes, expensive shoes, that kind of thing."

Joel smiled. "Exactly. Now, think about what we are experiencing right now. No electricity, cars don't run, electronics don't work ... what do you think is going to happen in a few days after the stores have been looted and the food is gone? I'm pretty sure nobody shopped for groceries for the next year or more. In a few days, maybe a week, people are going to be looking for other sources for food and water. Hell, there might be some of them who have already figured out this isn't going to be over soon and are already doing that. If the stores are empty, where's the next logical place to look for food?"

Shocked, she replied, "Houses. Most people have food in their houses. Most of them probably have a whole lot more than I do. Oh wow. You think people would really

47

break in here to steal food … which I have very little of anyway?"

Sadly, Joel nodded. "I do. What would you do, if Aaron and Cameron were here, and you had no food for them?"

"We'd walk to your house."

He chuckled. "Okay. What if we didn't live so close? What if we were as far away as Elliott lives?"

Carly started to cry. "Please don't tell me we can't get to them, Dad. We have to get there. Elliott told me if anything ever happened, to get to his place, all of us; to use a back way through Arlington. Maybe he meant up Highway 14. I don't know, but I have to be with my boys!"

Joel reached over and pulled her into his arms. "We will get there, honey. It won't be today, it may not be for a few days. But we'll get there, I promise. In the meantime, Elliott will watch out for them. You know he will."

Carly cried on her dad's shoulder for a good five minutes. Her boys were thirty minutes away driving time. How long would it take her to walk that far? Could she walk that far? Yes, for her kids, she'd do it or die trying. She leaned back, wiped her eyes with the back of her sleeve, and took a deep breath. "Okay, Dad. I still don't understand all of this, but I trust you. Tell me what we need to do."

He smiled and said, "Let's load up the wagon."

The run back to Joel and Lauri's was much different. Many of the neighbors had jumped on the bandwagon and had their riding mowers out and fired up to verify that those would indeed work. They received waves and thumbs up from everyone who was out with their own riding mower. Carly and Joel laughed and waved back. They again pulled into the garage and unloaded their supplies. Once they were done, Joel wanted to put the mower back in the shed. He and Carly were arguing as he drove the mower into the backyard.

"Carly, you don't need your work clothes," Joel said as he was putting the lawn tractor back in the shed. She wanted to go back for one more load that consisted of the things she wore to work. The majority of their winter wear was at his house now. She had even grabbed the Christmas presents from under the tree and her briefcase and brought them along as well.

"But what if someone breaks in and steals them? You said that could happen, people breaking in. What would I wear to work then?"

"You won't be going to work anymore, honey. At least not for quite a while."

"What? If I don't go to work, how am I going to get paid?" she asked incredulously.

Joel sighed, then calmly said, "Okay, how are you going to get to work?"

Carly started to reply, paused, then didn't answer. Joel went on. "Right, you can't get there. If you could get there, what would you do?"

"Well, I could ..." She stopped. Everything she did was computerized. "Oh."

"Uh huh. And since everything is direct deposit and done electronically, how are you, or me, or anyone else going to get paid?"

She stood there dumbfounded. "What about my house payment? If I can't get paid, there won't be money in my account to send in my house payment, and I'll lose my house!"

Joel shook his head. "You're just not grasping the situation, honey. Everything electronic is gone. No more deposits. Unfortunately, no access to checking or savings accounts. All that money we had in savings is unavailable, maybe just gone."

49

"What do you mean it's gone? It's still there — we just can't get to it right now. Oh, and I have five hundred dollars cash on me. Will told me to get some out of the bank. Boy, am I glad I listened to him."

"It's there for now. Who knows what the situation will be in a few years if they get everything back on? Will the records or the files still be there? Will it have just vanished into cyberspace? I guess we'll just have to make it till then to find out. I have my cash stash as well. We may need it soon. Let's go inside and see how your mother's soup is coming along. I think I worked up an appetite."

Dejectedly, Carly followed her dad up to the house. *No job? No paycheck, no promotion, no profit sharing. I wonder what Marcus is doing right now? I don't think I'd want to be stuck in the Colorado mountains for something like this. What am I going to do? What are* we *going to do, everybody?* All of this was running through her mind as they walked in the house through the back door. Once inside, they could hear Lauri talking to someone, a male. They came around the corner into the living room and saw a young couple standing in the foyer with her. It was their new neighbors from across the street, Chris and Julie Jackson. They had only been living there about a month. Lauri took them a batch of cookies as a welcome gift the day they were moving in. Chris was talking.

"Oh, hi, Joel. Carly, right? Your mom and dad told us about you." Chris was stepping forward to shake Joel's hand as he addressed Carly.

"Morning, Chris, Julie. What's up?"

Lauri turned to her husband. "They were wondering if we could spare some firewood."

Chris chimed in. "We haven't had a chance to go out and get any wood what with the unpacking and getting settled. That wasn't a problem as long as we had electricity. It'd just be until we get through this cold snap. I'd be more than happy to replace it when everything comes back on. It's really cold in the house now."

Joel looked at the young couple then his wife. He could tell by the look in her eye that she wanted to help them. He turned back to Chris with a small smile. "We can probably spare some. Not a lot, but enough to warm your living room up at least. Do you have a chain saw?"

Chris shook his head. "No, this is our first house. I've never even used a chain saw before. I'd probably cut an arm or leg off." He laughed, Julie giggled, while Lauri and Carly smiled.

"I think I have an old one in the shed I can let you use," Joel said. "It's not big, but it will cut logs or trees no bigger than a foot across. It should work on those trees in your backyard."

"What? You want us to cut down our trees?" Julie exclaimed. "Why in the world would we do that? Some of those ornamentals are worth hundreds of dollars."

Joel replied matter-of-factly, "So you don't freeze to death."

Julie looked from Joel to Chris. Chris said, "Uh, we just wanted to borrow some firewood. We just need to get through today, maybe tomorrow. I don't think we need to go cutting down our trees."

Joel shrugged. "Suit yourself. One sec." He went to the hearth and picked up half a dozen split logs of the dozen or so that were stacked there. He took them and handed them to Chris. "These will probably last you an hour, maybe two. When they're gone, I don't know what y'all are going to do. We don't have a lot ourselves, and I'll likely be cutting down a tree here soon. It'll be green, but if the fire is hot enough, it'll burn; slow, but it'll do the job. If you change your mind about cutting your own, let me know. I'll lend you the saw and show you how to use it."

51

Chris took the wood and smiled at them. "I don't think that will be necessary but thank you for the offer. I'll let you all get back to your day. Something smells wonderful, by the way."

"Oh, let me get you both some soup to take with you," Lauri said. She hurried to the kitchen and in just a minute came back with a large plastic container of her homemade vegetable soup. She also had something wrapped in paper towels, as well as a small egg carton. She handed it to Julie. "There's some cornbread there as well. Tricky making it in a camping oven but I figured it out. I also put a half-dozen eggs in from my chickens."

"Oh, thank you, Lauri! This is wonderful!" Julie replied. "I didn't know what we were going to do about cooking. We have an electric stove, too. Oh, and thank you for the eggs, but I just can't bring myself to eat them if they don't come from the grocery store. I just feel safer when they've passed all the governmental requirements." She handed the small carton back to Lauri.

Lauri took the carton from her and smiled at them. "Alrighty then. Well, you should eat it while it's hot. I don't think it will stay that way for long in this weather."

Chris nodded. "We're going to do that right now. Thank you again, for everything!"

Joel held the door as they left. When he had closed it behind them, he turned to his family. "I think we need to talk. Let's eat and we'll talk over lunch."

Carly and Lauri looked at each other. Carly shrugged as they followed Joel into the kitchen.

Chapter 7

Elliott woke with a start. He sat up in bed, trying to figure out what woke him. It didn't dawn on him at first — not until he looked at the alarm clock to see what time it was. The display was blank. *Huh. Power must be out. Probably ice on the lines.* He got up to relieve himself and check things out. With no power, his well was off, which meant the toilet had one flush. He decided to take care of his business outside.

He donned coat, hat, and boots over his long underwear and stepped out the back door. His ranch-style house had a front and back porch the length of the house. Part of the back porch was closed in as a utility room, which held a large chest freezer, among other things.

Still a few hours from sunrise, it was pitch black outside with the cloud cover from the winter storm. It didn't matter. He knew his way around the place like the back of his hand. He walked to the end of the porch and emptied his bladder. By the time he was done, his eyes had adjusted to the darkness. He could make out the small pole barn that housed his goats and chickens. He could hear some rustling coming from inside. Perhaps he had disturbed them when he came out and let the screen door slam shut. He walked over to the steps and found they were indeed covered in a layer of ice and snow. *Have to get some rock salt on that when the sun comes up,* he thought.

Going back inside, he went to the living room and stoked the fire in the wood-burning stove. Once it was going well, he took a kerosene lamp from the mantle and lit it. The soft glow filled the dark room. He went to his bedroom and dug into the top drawer of his dresser. His father's old pocket watch was wrapped lovingly in a

53

handkerchief that had also belonged to the man. Elliott wound it a few times and it started ticking. He wound the watch the rest of the way, then slipped on a pair of pants and a flannel shirt as he headed to the kitchen, picking up the lantern on the way and sticking the watch in his pocket.

The table in the corner of the large farm-style kitchen had belonged to his grandmother. It was very old and had been used to feed many people, many times. It was made of plank wood that had been scoured so much it was shiny. Elliott kept a tablecloth on it to protect the wood. The added bonus was the storage space underneath. He pulled the tablecloth up and pulled out a five-gallon water jug from under it. There were five more just like it under the table, all filled with water from his well. He set the jug on the counter, then turned it on its side so the spout was accessible. He opened the cabinet next to the stove and pulled out a stove-top percolator. He filled the pot with water from the jug, added coffee to the basket, and placed it on the gas stove. He turned the burner on under the pot then went to the dining table and sat down to wait. He pulled the watch out of his pocket and set it to the battery-operated clock above the stove, which read four thirty.

He was on his third cup when Aaron shuffled into the kitchen. It was still dark out, but he could see the sky lightening slightly through the window over the sink. Aaron rubbed his eyes as he sat down at the table with his grandfather. Elliott smiled at the memory of his son, Ethan, doing the same thing years ago. They looked so much alike it was like stepping back in time for him. Elliott got up and took another coffee cup from the hanger beside the sink.

"Morning, son. You want some coffee?"

Aaron nodded. "Morning. Sure, thanks, Pap. You have sugar and creamer?"

Elliott snorted. "Yeah, I got sugar, but you'll have to settle for goat's milk for your cream. I don't taint my coffee with any fixins'. Straight black for me."

Aaron rolled his eyes and motioned with his head to the lantern on the table. "That's fine. What's up with the lights? Is the power out?"

"Yep. I've been up for a couple of hours and it was off then. Probably ice on the lines or a tree fell over on them or something." Elliott handed him the cup of steaming coffee. "Sugar is on the counter, milk in the fridge. Make it quick, don't want to let too much cold out."

Aaron stood up. "Okay, I'm gonna go to the bathroom first."

"Hold up, Aaron. We're gonna have to go outside to pee until the power comes back on. Remember, I'm on a well. If the power goes out, we have no water in the house. No water, no toilet flushing. You can go off the porch until the sun comes up. We'll find a spot a bit away from the house if the power doesn't come back on here in a bit. Best grab your coat. It's cold out there."

"Um … okay. Peeing outside. Haven't done that since I was a kid out here," Aaron said, grinning.

"One of those times it's good to be a guy, huh?" Elliott laughed as he sat back down.

"If you say so, Pap. If there were girls here, they wouldn't have to go outside to pee."

Elliott looked at his grandson for a moment, then replied, "You've got a point there, kiddo. Maybe we got the short end of that stick after all."

Aaron chuckled as he got up to go get his coat. "I better get Cam up and let him know not to use the toilet either. Be back in a sec."

Elliott stood up again. "Guess we should get some breakfast going, too. We'll need to haul in more wood and probably get some more water hauled in here. Just in case." He went over to the pantry and started pulling things out.

Aaron walked down the hall and into the room he shared with his brother when they stayed with their grandfather. He leaned over and shook Cameron. "Cam. Wake up."

Cameron groaned and pulled the blanket over his head. "Go away. It's too early."

"You don't even know what time it is," Aaron replied.

Cameron uncovered one eye and peered at his brother. "Since I can barely see you, it's still dark, which means it's too early." He covered his head back up.

Aaron picked up his coat and slipped it on. "Fine. Just don't pee in the bathroom. The power's off. You have to pee out back, off the porch." He reached for his cell phone on the night stand.

"What? What does the power have to do with the toilet?" Cameron asked, uncovering his whole head to look at Aaron.

"The well is electric. No water." Aaron was peering at his phone, pushing buttons and tapping the screen. "Huh. That's weird. I could have sworn I charged my cell before we left the house. Great. My battery is crapping out now."

"Here, use mine," Cameron said as he picked his own up from the bedside. "No way! Mine's dead, too! I just charged it last night. What the hell?"

Aaron shrugged. "No idea. I gotta take a leak. Pap's getting breakfast going. C'mon, you're awake now, you might as well get up."

Cameron huffed as he threw the covers to the side. "Alright, alright, hang on, I'll go with you."

Cameron put his coat on and they both donned their winter boots over bare feet. As they traipsed through the kitchen, Cameron called out, "Morning, Pap. Going to

56

shake the dew off the lily. Outside. In the cold. Be right back."

Standing at the stove, Elliott turned and grinned at him. "Morning, Cam. Y'all hurry up. Oatmeal will be ready in a jiffy." He turned back and stirred the pot.

The boys walked out onto the porch and stopped. The sky was lightening, though they couldn't see the sun from the cloud cover. The ground, the trees, the outbuildings — everything they could see was covered in a thin layer of ice, which was being covered by the steady snow falling. The little bit of light that got through the clouds was making the ice glisten. It was snowing, and the scene was amazing, even to two teenage boys.

"Wow!" exclaimed Cameron. "That is bee-yoo-tee-full." He enunciated each syllable like a separate word.

"Yep, pretty cool. But damn, it's cold. C'mon, let's get done and get back inside."

They took care of their business, even with Cameron playing around — "Look! I made a smiley face in the snow!" — and hurried back into the warmth of the house. Elliott had three bowls of oatmeal set out on the table with honey, cinnamon, dried apples, butter, and milk.

"Eat up, fellas, we got work to do," he said as he sat down in front of his own bowl.

Cameron whined, "Work? I thought we were gonna shoot, Pap." He added honey and cinnamon to his oatmeal.

Elliott nodded and spoke around a mouthful. "We are, but we've got to do a few chores first. Living in the country ain't like it is in Memphis. A power outage out here could take a while to fix, depending on what caused it. That layer of ice I saw on the trees from the window could have broken limbs, which fall on the power lines and pull them off the poles. If there's a bunch down, it could take a few days to get them all fixed. We need to bring a bunch of wood up from the shed and fill up some more water jugs at

57

the pump. We can pee off the porch; the other, we're gonna need water to flush the toilets for. We can throw some of the ash from the stove out there where we're peeing so it don't stink.

"We need to get a couple of coolers and put the milk and sandwich stuff in them and put them out in the utility room with the freezer. They'll be better off out there as cold as it is. There's some rock salt in there, too. We need to spread it on the steps to melt that ice off. Don't need anybody breaking a hip slipping down the steps. Namely, me."

"Okay, Pap," Cameron said with a sigh. "We'll do it as soon as we get done eating."

Aaron said, "Pap, can I use your phone? Mine's dead and so is Cam's. Weird, too, because we both thought we had them charged. I wanted to call and check on Mom, see if the power is out there, too."

"Sure, let me go get it off the dresser," Elliott replied as he got up from the table. "She's probably fine though."

"I'll get it. You finish your breakfast." Aaron stood up and took his bowl to the sink. He tried to turn the faucet on then laughed. "No water, genius," he chided himself aloud.

"Use some out of that jug there on the counter," Elliott said. "We'll heat some water on the stove and wash them up good after we get everything else done outside. Maybe make a pot of hot cocoa."

Aaron opened the valve on the jug and let the water run into his bowl. "It's kind of like a sink faucet, huh? When did you get these jugs, Pap?"

"A few years ago. I saw them at Walmart in the camping section. Seemed like a pretty good idea for storing up some water. Even got a couple on sale because they were dented. I'd buy one every month or so until I had enough to store under Granny's old table over there." He pointed to the table in the corner. "Six fit under there perfect and hold enough water to keep me for about a month without even leaving the house — as long as I pee outside. We'll empty that one into some pots and pitchers, so we can refill it while we're out."

Cameron walked over to the old table and pulled the tablecloth aside. "I used to crawl in here and pretend this was an indoor fort when I was a little kid. I haven't looked under here in years. Nice hidey hole, Pap."

"Yep. Figured it was a good spot since you weren't using it anymore," Elliott said with a laugh. "Well, let's get a move on, boys. I also need to milk the goats and gather eggs. Lots to do, so we might as well get to doing it."

Aaron walked into Elliott's bedroom and picked up his cell phone. It was an old flip phone, with no internet, no texting, nothing fancy at all. He opened it and found a small blank screen. He took it to Elliott.

"So, no one has a charged cell phone? This is nuts!"

Elliott took the phone. He opened it, pushed buttons, but got no response from the device. "This ain't right. I just charged it yesterday when we got back from your house. My battery lasts for days. There's something going on here." He went to the phone hanging on the wall. He picked up the receiver. It was dead. "Definitely something going on. The reason I've kept this phone all these years is because it works when the power is out and there's no battery to run down. So, why ain't it working?"

He looked at the boys. Cameron shrugged. "Maybe a tree fell on the phone line, too. We should go out and look around."

Elliott nodded. "Yeah. Let's do that. First, let's empty that jug."

They filled everything they could with water from the container. Elliott set four pots on the stove and turned them down on low. "That should be hot enough to wash dishes in by the time we get done outside. Let's go."

It took them about an hour to get everything done. The snow switched to sleet and back to snow again a few times, with some kind of frozen precipitation falling continuously. They checked the lines coming to the house; nothing was disconnected. When they had finished the chores, Elliott took his keys off a hook by the back door.

"I'm gonna go out to the truck and see if there's anything on the radio about this mess. You boys warm up and get some wash water going for those breakfast dishes. I'll be right back." Elliott went out to his truck, a 1999 Chevy Silverado, which sat under the detached carport. He climbed in and put the key in the ignition. When he turned the key to the "On" position, nothing happened. No dash lights, no radio, nothing. He turned it on to "Start" with the same results. He tried it a couple of times, but it was dead. He popped the hood and looked underneath. Nothing seemed out of place. The battery was there. He moved the cables back and forth to check that they were tight. He went back to the cab and tried one more time. Not even a click. He sat there looking at the dark console, trying to work it out in his head.

No electricity in the house. The phones aren't working. My truck won't start. This is bad, real bad. He got out of his truck, put the hood down, and went back into the house.

Aaron and Cameron had washed the dishes and were sitting in the living room staring at the glass front of the wood stove, sipping their hot chocolate. Elliott opened the back door into the kitchen. He shook his coat out and hung it on a hook on the door. Aaron got up off the couch and went to the kitchen to make him a cup of cocoa as well.

"Well, Pap? What'd you find out? Did they say how far it spreads or when the power might be back on?" he asked, as he handed the warm cup to his grandfather.

Elliott took the cup and went to the kitchen table. "Boys, come in here. We need to talk and get some plans made."

Confused but curious, the two boys did as their grandfather requested and joined him at the table. Cameron asked, voice full of concern, "What is it, Pap? What's wrong?"

Elliott stared into his cup for a moment, then looked at his grandsons. "I'm not sure, Cam, but it's something bad. My truck won't start. Won't even turn over. It's like there's no battery in it. Before you ask, I checked and it's there. There's no way that battery is bad. I just got it a couple of months ago. I started adding it all up — the electricity, the phones, the truck — this ain't just a power outage."

"Then what is it?" Aaron asked, anxiously.

Elliott looked thoughtful. "I'm not entirely sure. But I think it might be something like an EMP."

The boys were quiet. After a moment, Cameron spoke up. "Okay, I'll bite. What's an EMP?"

Aaron replied, "It stands for electromagnetic pulse. We studied it in advanced science. Basically, it's a burst of energy that radiates through the air and fries everything electrical. And it would definitely explain everything that's not working now. Holy crap — do you really think that's it, Pap? I mean, now that I think about it, it makes sense."

Elliott nodded slowly. "I do. I've heard about them, heard what people think would happen if a big one hit. Just never figured it would."

"Wow! This is unreal," Aaron exclaimed. "I wonder how big it was, how it happened ... you know, what caused it. It couldn't have been a sun spot. We'd have heard about it days ago."

"I don't know but this sure changes things," Elliott replied. "Boys, if that's what this is, we're in for some hard times ... and it may be a while before you see your mom again."

Cameron sat up straight, his voice laced with concern and a bit of panic. "What do you mean, Pap? Why can't we see Mom? Is she all right?"

Elliott placed his hand on his grandson's arm. "Calm down, Cam. I'm sure she's fine. It's just — well, we can't get to her and she can't get here. Not right away, anyway. But she's got your grandparents close, and I'm sure Joel will see that she's safe. And I'm gonna make sure you guys are safe right here. I told her if anything happened, they should all come here, and I know they'll do that just as soon as they can. In the meantime, we're gonna do what we can to stay warm and fed. Aaron, get me that pad and paper in the living room by my chair. We need to start planning."

Aaron went to the living room and brought the requested items back. "What are we planning, Pap?"

Elliott tore off the top sheet to reveal a clean one. "How to live without electricity."

Chapter 8

The Pentagon

"He's insane. He's totally lost it. He can't do this!" General Everley was pacing the conference room connected to his office like a caged animal. Admiral Stephens watched Everley, shaking his head.

"Agreed, but how do we stop him? We're at war. The country will be in complete chaos as soon as the people realize the power isn't coming back on any time soon. Do we attempt a coup in the middle of this shit?"

Everley stopped his pacing. "Who said anything about a coup?"

Stephens shrugged. "Sounded like that's where you were headed. I'm not really sure what our options are at this point. Either we follow the orders of the commander in chief," he said, rolling his eyes, "or we go AWOL. Personally, I think I'll go with the latter."

Everley looked at him wide-eyed. "Are you serious? You'd risk your career, your pension, or worse, prison? You would abandon your post during a time of war?"

Stephens smirked at Everley, then replied, "My career? My pension? Have you even considered the gravity of the situation we're in? It will take years — God only knows how many — to get power restored to this country. Olstein's plan, if you can call it that, is to turn this constitutional republic into a communist dictatorship. As of today, my pension is gone and so is yours. The Bill of Rights and the Constitution are being shredded as we speak. Repeal the Second Amendment? Not giving up the White House? You're wrong, he's not insane; he's fucking brilliant. He's taking the worst situation this country has ever seen and turning it into a win, for him anyway. And the people, the citizens of this great land? The majority of them will be so freaked out by what's going on they'll let it happen — probably encouraging him to do so for the promises of food, shelter, and security. The ones who don't, the patriots who know the value of their freedom and their rights, will be labeled as rebels and enemies of the state.

"I don't know about you, but I will not go to war against my own people, especially the ones fighting for our rights and our freedom. I will not hunt down individuals because they do not agree with the current administration's ideas for what this country *should* be, rather than what it *is*. I'd rather fight by their side … because that's the right side. I'm five years past retirement anyway. I've more than earned the right to step down."

Stephens rose and walked over to where Everley stood staring at him. He reached out his hand. "Good luck, Charles. I'm going to take the Hummer assigned to me and go pick up my wife. Then, we're going to try to get to my brother's place in the Smokies. You're welcome to join us. 'There's safety in numbers' is not just a saying."

Everley looked like he was considering the offer; then, he shook his head. "No, I can't go. Someone needs to stay here, to try to keep some semblance of order around here and this administration in check. Good luck to you, too, Arthur. May we never meet across the battlefield."

Stephens shook his head. "Don't go to war for him, Charles. Remember your oath. You swore to defend the Constitution against all enemies foreign and domestic, not be a puppet for a dreaming dictator. Don't fight your own people. If it comes to that, leave when you can."

"Okay, I'll try. Be safe," Everley said as he released the admiral's hand and stepped back. He came to attention and snapped a salute to his long-time friend. Stephens returned it.

"You do the same, Charles. God bless." With that, Stephens walked out of the room. Everley watched him leave, feeling as if he had let an opportunity slip by. He sighed.

"You're in it now, Chucky boy," he said aloud. "Let's see where this crazy train leads us."

~~~~~

Arthur went straight to the townhouse he and his wife owned in Georgetown. He parked on the street out front and hurried into their home, calling out to his wife, Jean, as he unlocked the door.

"Jean? Where are you?"

"In the kitchen, dear. Be right there," she called from the back of the house.

Arthur didn't wait for her to come to him. He walked through the kitchen door with a purpose she could see in his stride. She looked up and smiled.

"Or you could come to me," she teased. Seeing the grim look on his face, she asked, "What's wrong? What was the big meeting about?"

He walked over to her, took his wife by the arm, and led her to the kitchen table. Sitting down beside her, he tried to explain to her what had happened and what was going on. The longer he talked, the more wide-eyed and concerned she became.

"I don't understand, Art. You're saying the power is not going to come back on?" she asked incredulously, "and we're leaving Washington to go to your brother's place in Tennessee? It's been at least ten years since you've seen or spoken to him. How do you even know if he still lives there? And why do we have to leave our home?"

65

Arthur rubbed his eyes, then let his hands continue down his face. "Because everything is going to go to hell really quick, Jeannie. When people find out the power isn't coming back on for a long time, anarchy will be the theme of the day. There will be mass looting, particularly at the grocery stores, and lawlessness will reign. There's over half a million people in DC alone. When the food is gone — and it will be, probably in about a week — the people will panic and do whatever they have to do to feed themselves and their families. The police won't be around because they'll be trying to feed their own families. Besides that, they're not going to work for free, and I'm pretty sure no one's getting paid again for a long time. And on top of all this, the *president*," he said with a sneer, "wants to shred the Constitution, steal from the people, and keep the White House, apparently for good. This place is going to become a war zone very soon. We can't be here when that happens. We have to go. Philip will be there. I'd know if he wasn't."

Jean sat staring at him, shock apparent in her expression. She looked around her beautiful modern kitchen, where nothing worked at the moment, then back to her husband. In a soft voice, barely above a whisper, she said, "But how will we live with no money, no home, and no food? We'll be in the same position as everyone else, won't we?"

Arthur shook his head and gave her a small smile. "No, we won't, because we know what happened; we know what's going to happen; and we're not going to be here when it does. We're going to be in a place where people live more simply, back to the basics." He stood, pulling her into his arms. They stayed like that for a few minutes, Jean sobbing softly into her husband's chest. When the tears seemed to be subsiding, Arthur held her away from him and said, "Okay, we've got about four hundred miles to get to Philip's place. We need to get some bags packed and get

66

moving. Pack warm, sturdy clothes; all the soap, shampoo, hand sanitizer, those kinds of things you can get in one bag; any food we can eat as is — you know, that doesn't need to be cooked or heated — as well as any bottle or canned drinks."

She stopped him. "It's only a six–hour drive, Art. We shouldn't need all the drinks in the house."

"Depending on what it's like out there, it may take us a lot longer than six hours to get there. There will be dead vehicles all over the roads. There will be people who were in those vehicles, either still in them, or trying to make their way somewhere else. This won't be the straight drive down I-81 we used to make years ago. Right now, we don't even know if we can use I-81. Let's pack like we might not be able to." He leaned down and kissed her on her forehead. "I need to go pack a few things myself. I'll catch up with you in a few minutes to see how you're doing."

She nodded and watched as he walked down the hall and started up the stairs. When she could no longer see him, Jean started pulling chips and snacks out of the cabinets and setting them on the counter top. She stopped, looked around the kitchen, then into the dining room. The china cabinet was filled with dishes from her mother and grandmother. The sideboard held pictures of their children and grandchildren who were in Texas. Would Art take her to them? Could they get that far? Tears started down her face as she walked into the dining room and gathered the framed photos of her family. She took them back to the kitchen and wrapped them in dish towels, placing them in the bottom of a reusable shopping bag, then setting the chips in on top of them. She wiped her face and continued gathering food from the kitchen she might never see again. At that thought, the tears started anew.

Arthur went up to his office and closed the door. He went to the bookcase on the wall and pulled out a three-book section, which was covering a panel that looked no different from the rest of the wall — that is, to anyone else. He pressed lightly on the panel until he heard a click inside the wall. Grasping the shelf, he pulled the bookcase section toward him. It opened like a door and revealed a wall with various handguns, rifles, and shotguns mounted to it. He started pulling the weapons from the wall and laying them on the furniture in the room. Drawers below the guns held hundreds of rounds of ammunition for each one. He pulled those out as well.

He stepped out into the hall and went to the linen closet at the end. He pulled his sea bag out of the bottom and took it back to his office. He loaded the guns and ammunition into the bag and carried it to the hall, except for the Colt 1911 .45, which he placed in his waistband. He left the bag beside his office door, where the weight of it created a thunk. Living in D.C., where gun ownership was all but outlawed, meant making some concessions. However, he had never, and would never, give up his right to own them. He just got creative in the way he stored them. He didn't have nearly as many as he would have liked to have had in a situation like this and nowhere near enough ammo. But it would have to do. His brother, Philip, would be well-stocked ... they just had to get there.

Next, Arthur went to a wall safe across the room. Turning the dial quickly, he unlocked it and opened the door. From inside, he pulled their passports, birth certificates, marriage license, and two thousand dollars in cash. He knew the cash was probably worthless, but not everyone else did. Not yet, at least. He hoped it would be enough to get them to Tennessee. Both of them were in their late fifties; both had high blood pressure and were on medication for it. They were probably fit enough to walk a few miles over flat ground, but no way they could hike mountains. He wondered how long it would be before one of them had a stroke or a heart attack once the blood pressure medicine was gone. He walked to the landing and called downstairs.

"Jeannie, don't forget our medications, headache meds, vitamins — just empty that shelf into the bag as well."

"Okay, getting all that now," she called back, trying to hide the fact that she had been crying.

He went to their bedroom, set the pistol on the chest, and took off his uniform. He was pretty sure he had just worn it for the last time. He laid it respectfully on the bed and removed the ribbon bars from the chest. He pulled a duffel bag from the top of the closet and placed the ribbon bars in the side pocket. Donning jeans and a Navy sweatshirt, he added more jeans, a couple of sweaters, some flannel shirts, socks and underwear, as well as tennis shoes and hiking boots to the bag. He put on a pair of tactical boots, placed the pistol in the back waistband, and carried the duffel to the hall, setting it beside his sea bag. He pulled one more pair of pants and a shirt from his chest of drawers and stuck them in the top of his sea bag to cover the contents. Pulling the drawstring tight, he took a moment to catch his breath.

By this time, Jean had packed up what she thought they should take from the kitchen and had come upstairs to pack their clothes. Seeing the bags sitting in the hall, she looked at Arthur.

"Looks like you've been busy, too," she said. "I'm guessing you took care of the supplies from your office."

He nodded. "Yes, and I packed my clothes as well. All you need to do is pack clothes for yourself and get the stuff from the bathroom. Unless you want me to get that."

"No, I'll take care of it. It won't take but a few minutes. Besides, shouldn't you be loading up the car?" she asked.

"Yes ma'am, I should, and I will," he replied. "Let me know if you need any help up here." He picked up the two bags, slung one over each shoulder, and headed down the stairs.

In a world where most of the vehicles were not running, the Humvee had garnered some attention from the neighbors when he pulled up. A few were standing outside his front door, looking at the vehicle and talking to each other. When Arthur opened the door, all heads turned towards him.

One of his neighbors, Craig Duff, addressed him from the sidewalk. "Hey, Art. How come your ride works when nobody else's does?"

Arthur hesitated at the top of the stairs. He knew this was going to happen at some point, but he wasn't prepared for it to happen right then. Explaining why the Hummer still ran was simple; explaining why he was loading up bags and wearing civilian clothes, not so much. He continued down the stairs resolutely and joined the group at the bottom.

"Well, Craig, all I can tell you is it was stored in a garage underground, so maybe that protected it from whatever happened up here." He opened the back window and put the bags inside, being careful to set his sea bag down gently so it didn't make much noise.

Craig went on. "Oh, I see. If you're a bigwig in the government, you get special treatment. You'll be riding around town while us peons are walking everywhere," he remarked disdainfully. "What the hell is going on here anyway? I'm sure you know, being an admiral and all."

Arthur heaved a heavy sigh, then turned to Craig. "I'm sorry your car doesn't run, Craig. I wish I could help you, but I can't. Honestly, I don't know much more than you do. Now, if you'll excuse me, I need to finish loading this truck, so Jean and I can get on the road."

Belligerently, Craig barked, "Yeah? Where are you off to in such a hurry? You do know something, don't you? Tell us, dammit! We have a right to know, too!"

Arthur stepped up until he was chest to chest with Craig. He replied softly, "I don't like your tone, Craig. Where I'm going is none of your concern. I would suggest you step back and let me get on with my business. In fact, you should go on home and take care of your family. I don't know what's going on, but I have a feeling dark days are coming. You should go get ready for them."

With that, Arthur closed and locked the back of the Humvee, headed back up the steps, went inside, and shut the door behind him. He went upstairs to their bedroom and found Jean zipping up the bag she had filled from the bathroom. On the bed lay two suitcases full of clothes that hadn't yet been closed. He walked over and started zipping up the closest one.

"Are you ready? We've got a situation developing out front. We need to get out of here as soon as we can." He was reaching for the second suitcase as he spoke. "I'll take these down to the front door, but I'm going to wait a few minutes to see if the people out front move along before I take anything else outside. How much do you have in the kitchen that needs to go out?"

"Four of the reusable grocery bags and the big cooler. I also dumped the ice from the icemaker in on top of the things in the cooler. What's going on outside?" she asked as she followed him down the stairs.

"A bunch of looky-loos wondering why the Humvee works and their cars don't," Arthur told her. "And we don't have time for me to explain the damage an EMP does or what their lives are about to become. We need to get out of town right now."

He went to the front window and peered out. Most of the onlookers had left. Craig was still there, with another

71

man Arthur did not know. He turned to Jean and said, "I'm going to take those two suitcases out. Stay here. You can go ahead and bring the bags from the kitchen and set them in the hallway. I'll be right back."

She nodded as he opened the door, picked up the bags, set them on the stoop, and closed the door behind him. At the sound of the door opening, Craig and his friend looked up at Arthur. As he carried the suitcases down the stairs, the two men watched him closely.

"Wow, looks like you folks are going on an adventure," Craig remarked in a snarky tone. "Wish my car was running so I could go on one, too."

Arthur unlocked the back of the Humvee and placed the suitcases inside the storage area. Closing and locking it again, he turned to the men, slipping his hands into the back pockets of his jeans.

"I thought I told you that you should go on home, Craig. This is none of your concern, as I've already said. Now, get out of my face."

"You can't tell me what to do! This is a free country. I'm just standing on the sidewalk; you don't own the sidewalk. I'm pretty sure my tax dollars paid for that vehicle. I'm just wondering if wherever you're going is official business, old man, especially since you're taking your wife," Craig said smugly, standing in front of Arthur, blocking his path.

Arthur slid his right hand from his back pocket onto the pearl-handled grips of the Colt in his waistband. "Get out of my way, Craig. Don't make me say it again."

"Or what? Are you threatening me, *Admiral*?"

"No, I'm telling you. Get ..." He pulled the gun from his waistband. "Out ..." They heard the hammer cock as he brought the gun to bear. "Of my way, asshole."

Craig and his buddy stumbled backwards at the sight of the gun, Craig tripping over the curb and landing in the slushy snow in the grass beside the street. He scrambled up and ran off, watching Arthur over his shoulder, yelling, "He's got a gun! Somebody call the cops!"

Arthur chuckled as he watched them run. "Yes, by all means, call the cops! Oh wait — no phones!" he called out after them. Problem resolved, he went back to get Jean and the rest of the things.

They loaded up the last of it, locked the front door, and climbed into the Humvee. When the engine started, Jean could see her neighbors peering out through their curtains at the sound, but no one else bothered them. Arthur reached over and took her hand. "Are you ready, Jeannie?"

She turned to him, a lone tear trickling down her cheek, and said, "Whither thou goest, I will go."

Chapter 9

Will walked along the highway, lost in his thoughts. *What could cause something like this? How far does it reach?* He had a feeling the answer to the last question was pretty far, if the way the sky lit up when it happened was any indication. These were things he needed to discuss with his dad, which caused him to pick up his pace a bit. His sense of urgency to get home increased with every step. He was so engrossed in analyzing the situation, he didn't realize someone was talking to him.

"Hey, buddy! Wait up!"

Will stopped and turned to see a woman with a large hiking pack on her back, bundled up in serious winter outerwear, hurrying toward him. She smiled as she got close.

"I was beginning to think maybe you were hearing impaired or something. I've been hollering at you for like ten minutes." She stood with her gloved hands hooked in the straps of her backpack. Will could see wisps of blonde hair sticking out of her toboggan, framing a face with the most captivating blue eyes he had ever seen. When she smiled, they sparkled like diamonds. He couldn't help but smile back and picked up on her Northern accent.

"Sorry, I was lost in my thoughts, thinking about how crazy this is. I see you had the same idea as me about heading out on foot."

"Yeah, I'm not really sure what this is, but I'm not the type to sit around waiting for someone to help me. I try to help myself. I decided to see if I can get ... I don't know, somewhere ... and crash for a few days. Doesn't look like I'm getting home any time soon."

"Where's home?" he asked.

"Wisconsin. A little town called Rhinelander. You've probably never heard of it."

Will's face lit up. "Are you kidding me? My dad is from Rhinelander!"

"No way! That is too cool! Imagine us meeting on the road like this — two people in Tennessee who actually know where Rhinelander, Wisconsin, is! I'm Amanda, by the way. Amanda Frye." She stuck out a gloved hand to Will.

"Will Chambers," he replied as he shook her hand. "Yeah, you probably aren't going to get nine hundred miles on foot. You're welcome to walk with me. I'm going to my folks' place in Bartlett. It's about one percent of the mileage you're looking at."

"Very nice to meet you, Will Chambers. I'd love to walk with you. Bartlett definitely works."

They started forward again. After a moment, Will picked up the conversation. "So, what is a Yankee gal from Northern Wisconsin doing down here anyway? No offense."

She chuckled. "None taken. I get that a lot. I go to Ole Miss. I was on my way home for Christmas break. Guess I should have left a day earlier, huh?"

He looked at her and said, "You're in college? I figured you were closer to my age. Oh, shit ... sorry, no offense ... again."

She laughed then. "Well, I probably should be offended on that one, but I actually am about your age. My dad died last year, cancer. He left me part of his estate on the stipulation I use some of it to go back to school to get my master's degree. I'm going for my master's in business."

He replied, "Nice. Speaking of nice, that's a killer rig you have there. Are you a hiker or something?"

She nodded. "Yep. I love hiking. Sometimes when I go, I lose track of time, so I keep a one-man tent, sleeping bag,

75

cooking setup, dried foods, a water filter, that kind of stuff, in my pack all the time. Whenever I go anywhere, my pack goes with me. You never know when the urge to hit the trail will come."

Will cocked his head at her. "Water filter?"

"Yeah, it's pretty cool actually. You can either scoop up water into a glass or some kind of container, stick the straw in, and drink, or you can use it straight from whatever water you can find."

"Like a puddle? That sounds kind of gross," Will replied with a grimace.

Amanda grinned. "The key word here is *filter*. It filters out all the baddies in the water, leaving you something safe to drink. That could come in handy if you find yourself running out of water."

"Have you tried it?"

"As a matter of fact, I have. Scooped up a bottle from a nasty puddle in the woods a couple of years ago. Filtered it into the pouch, it tasted fine — and I didn't die, obviously."

Now it was Will's turn to chuckle. "Obviously. Well, I am happy you came along, Amanda. You've made my day suck a little less."

She gave him a quick salute. "Glad I could be of service, sir!"

They shared a laugh and continued down the road.

As they walked, Will confided some of his thoughts about the event. She agreed that whatever it was, it was not your normal, everyday power outage, but she had no clue as to what could do something like this either. He didn't share the fact he had visions, or that he had experienced some regarding this situation. He did find her very easy to talk to, though. And those eyes …

"Hello? Anybody home?" she teased, leaning over to nudge him as they walked.

76

"Huh? Sorry, I guess my mind was wandering. What did you say?"

"I said I wonder how far I can get today, if I keep walking. I'm good on food and water for a few days anyway. I just don't know whether I should keep going as far as I can go or try to find a hotel or something. What do you think?"

He stopped and looked at her. He thought about the visions — the darkness, the people starving and freezing, some attacking others. He said, "I think you should come with me to my parents' house. I don't think you should be on the road alone, Amanda. I have a really bad feeling about this whole thing."

She looked at him wide-eyed. "Really? I don't want to impose, though. I'm sure I can find something ..."

"Do you have any cash on you?" he asked. "Not prying into your finances or anything, but if you don't have cash, you won't get a room, or any more food and stuff."

"Damn. I hadn't thought about that. No power means no credit cards work, and no I don't have a lot of cash. I hardly ever carry it. But still, shouldn't you ask your parents first? I mean, we're practically strangers, Will."

Will nodded. "I'm a pretty good judge of character. I believe you're a good person. Are you a good person, Amanda?"

"Well, I try to be," she replied. "I gave some of my food to a guy back there with four kids and a sick wife. I guess that constitutes being good."

"Yes, it does. My parents trust me, and I trust you. I have a feeling we're going to be a lot better acquainted by the time we get there, too. We still have a few miles to go."

Okay, how about we see how it goes on the trip. I may start getting on your nerves in about an hour or so."

He laughed. "I doubt it, but we can play it by ear. That's something I'm good at."

"I'm intrigued. Tell me more about yourself, Will Chambers." She linked a gloved hand through his arm and steered him toward their destination.

As they walked he told her about his job in Pigeon Forge. "Oh, a celebrity!" she exclaimed. "Are you famous? Should I know you?"

He snorted. "Not even remotely. I would have been suspicious if you had said you'd heard of us. But it's a good gig. When I first moved there, I was kind of glad to be that far from home, you know? Mom wouldn't just drop in without calling first to see if I had food and clean my apartment; Dad wouldn't be there all the time telling me how to do stuff. But the last couple of years, I find myself really missing them, and my sister and nephews. I've been thinking a lot about trying to find something closer to home."

"That would be nice for your mom and dad."

"Yeah. It's just really hard to leave the band. We've played together for five years. We get along great, no friction, no prima donnas. All the guys are talented. I don't know. Every time I make the drive home, it gets harder to leave. I've even limited my trips home to once a year, so I didn't have to deal with the dread. It doesn't help."

"Well, it sounds to me like you already know what you need to do, Will. I would suggest you start looking for something closer to home this trip — that is, if everything comes back on."

Will shook his head. "For some reason, I don't think a new gig is going to be high on my priority list for a little while. I don't know what this is, but I know it's bad. And I've got a feeling it's not getting fixed right away."

"Why do you say that?"

Will hesitated. *Should I tell her about the visions? How would I explain what I don't understand myself? No, not yet.* "Just because this isn't just a power outage, you know?

The cars, phones ... there's something else happening here. My dad was an electrical engineer before he retired. I bet he has an idea what's going on, maybe how to get through this. Let's keep going."

"Sounds like a plan, Will Chambers. Lead on," Amanda replied.

They didn't get too far before they were confronted by a woman climbing out of her car as they approached. She appeared to be in her mid-forties. She was dressed in a business suit with skirt and heels. She had a leather coat pulled tightly around her waist, but she was shivering nonetheless.

"Excuse me, do you know when the police or somebody will be coming to help us? It's been hours and I haven't seen anybody in authority. I've already missed my flight to Chicago this morning and I can't even reschedule since my phone died. Do either of you have a phone that's working?"

They both shook their heads as Will replied, "No, ma'am, I don't think anybody's phone is working. Do you have any warmer clothes you can put on? You look awfully cold."

"No, I don't. I was supposed to be flying out early for a quick meeting and then coming back home tonight. Just a day trip, you know? A high-profile client who, if he wants a meeting on Sunday, he gets a meeting on Sunday. I should have only needed my briefcase. And yes, I'm freezing." She shivered again as if to punctuate her remark.

"I wish I had something I could give you, but I literally have the clothes on my back," Amanda said. "Maybe someone around here ..." She turned to scan the area. This particular stretch of highway was emptier than some of the other parts Will, and probably Amanda, had walked through.

The woman shook her head. "Not really a lot of folks around, and I'm not walking anywhere in these shoes." She held her snow-covered pump up as evidence.

Amanda looked at Will, who gave her a quick head shake. He said, "Ma'am, I'm really sorry, but we just don't have any clothing to spare. I mean, I have a t-shirt and some boxers in my bag. Those aren't going to help you. The only thing I can suggest is you get into the back seat, curl up under your coat, and try to stay warm. You could maybe pull the floor mats up and lay them on top of your coat. We need to keep moving. Good luck, ma'am." He took Amanda by the arm and led her on down the road. He could hear the woman crying as they walked away.

Amanda let Will lead her for a bit then pulled her arm away. "Are we really going to do this? Just leave her here alone to freeze to death?"

Will stopped and turned to her. "What would you have me do, Amanda? She doesn't have any clothes or shoes that would make it possible for her to come with us. I don't have anything to give her. You don't either. So, what's our option?"

Amanda stood looking pensive, then crestfallen. "I guess you're right. How many people do you think are out there, right now, in the same situation as that poor woman? How many people were just going about their lives, heading to their jobs or home for the holidays and are now stranded, maybe hundreds of miles from home, possibly in the middle of nowhere, with no supplies and no means to get to any?"

"I don't know. Thousands. Maybe hundreds of thousands. The upside is it was the middle of the night … well, super early in the morning anyway. And it's Sunday. There weren't nearly as many people on the roads as there would have been tomorrow morning during rush hour. We don't know how widespread this is either. Nobody knows anything except that nothing works here." Will paused for a moment, then continued. "None of that matters to you and me right now. We need to get to my folks' house. We need shelter and some kind of food besides protein bars and beef jerky. I'm sorry we couldn't help her. We can't help anyone because we don't have anything to help them with. We just have to keep moving."

Amanda sighed. "I know you're right, Will. I just hate not helping people when they ask, if I can."

Will nodded. "Me too, Amanda. Unfortunately, in this situation, we can't. We have to focus on us now. And we really do need to keep moving. Are you ready?"

"Yes. Lead on," she replied, only this time the playful tone was gone. Will started down the road, Amanda following dejectedly. After a moment she said, "I feel like a total shitheel."

Will kept walking but turned his head and replied over his shoulder, "I've got a feeling we aren't even close to the level of shittiness we are going to feel today."

Chapter 10

Lauri cut the rest of the cornbread while Carly dished soup into bowls. They sat down with their food, Joel said grace, then Lauri looked at her husband. "What did you want to talk about, honey?"

Joel sighed. "Girls, we're going to have to decide who we're going to help and how much."

"I don't understand," she replied around a mouthful of soup.

"This situation is probably going to last for a while. Honestly, I can't fathom how long it's going to take to recover from it if it's very widespread. Have you heard any cars, trucks, helicopters, planes — any kind of moving vehicle? Besides the mower, of course."

Lauri considered the question. "Well, now that you mention it, I don't think I have."

Joel nodded slowly. "That's the part that concerns me. If it was just Memphis, even just the Mid-South, there would be helicopters flying over, checking the area, surveying the situation. There's nothing. I'm afraid this is going to be a long, hard road for everyone. That's why we are going to have to make some tough choices."

"What kind of choices, Dad?" Carly asked.

"We can't help everyone who comes to the door and asks for it. If we do, we'll run out of supplies ourselves. Then what?"

Carly looked thoughtful. "We find a way to get to Elliott's. He said we should come if Will's vision came true. I'm pretty sure it's come true."

"That's a good plan, honey, but we can't go right away. We need to give Will a chance to get home, for one thing," Joel said. "We'll also need to take stuff with us to Elliott's place. We can't show up empty-handed. So we need to try to conserve where we can. Unfortunately, that means not sharing with everyone who comes asking for help. That young couple just now? I guarantee you they'll be back, maybe as soon as tomorrow, looking for more wood, more food, something. They don't know anything about living without electricity."

Neither do I, Dad," Carly replied. "I'm completely lost. I've reached for my phone ten times today already." She held up her dead cell phone as evidence.

"Exactly. What would you be doing right now if I hadn't been here to tell you what I thought was happening?"

"Um … I dunno … probably bugging Stan to find out what's going on. Which would be no help at all."

"And how long would the food you had in your house last you?"

She grew wide-eyed. "Oh, wow, hmm. Well, if I ate the microwave food cold, or tried to heat it on the grill or something, and it was just me, maybe four, five days, a week at the most?"

Joel nodded again. "Okay. How many people live on your block? Just a guess."

Carly looked skyward as she counted in her head. "I don't know everybody, but there are eight to ten houses on each side, at least two people per house … say, something like forty, maybe sixty?"

"Call it sixty. So, what happens in a week when those sixty people run out of food?"

"Well, to be honest, Dad, I've been a slacker in the grocery department this week. I had every intention of stocking up on stuff yesterday, but the store was just …"

Joel smiled. "It's okay, honey. Just think about it. If everybody else had about the same amount of food as you, what happens in a week?"

"I guess they'd start looking for food somewhere else. They'd have to."

"Correct. So, in a polite society, people will first ask for help, like Chris and Julie did this morning. They were grateful for what we gave them, for the most part. What do you think is going to happen tomorrow, when the power is still off, and they still don't have wood to heat their home?"

"They'll come back here, asking for more. I would guess as time goes on they won't be nearly as picky about where things come from either," Lauri replied, glancing at the backyard eggs Julie had declined that were sitting on the table.

"Yep," Joel confirmed, "and they know we have wood and food. Now, we have to decide whether we will continue to help them or alienate them by declining. If we choose the latter, which we will have to do at some point, the situation changes. We are no longer helpful neighbors. We are the selfish people living across the street, hoarding their food, not helping their fellow man."

"So, what are you saying, Joel? We start turning people away? I don't know if I can do that," Lauri said. "We've been giving to our neighbors for years. We've shared fresh vegetables, as well as canned. Anyone who's lived here for any amount of time has received a part of our bounty. Are we supposed to sit by warm and fed while the people around us are cold and starving?"

Joel bowed his head, then looked at his wife sadly. "I hear you, honey. That's why I said we had some decisions to make. I just don't see how we can help everybody else and not starve ourselves."

Carly had sat quietly through their discussion. When her mother didn't comment right away, she spoke up. "What if we go ahead and put back what we want to take with us to Elliott's place? I mean, there's a lot of food here. Plus, Elliott has some really impressive food stores out

84

there. What we aren't planning to take Mom can share with the neighbors. Think about it, Dad. None of our vehicles run. How are we going to haul anything to Elliott's house? I don't see the riding mower carrying us out there, much less a bunch of supplies. We don't even know for sure if we can get there." Carly stopped, bottom lip trembling, obviously thinking about her boys.

Joel reached across the table and took Carly's hand. "We will get there, Carly. It won't be today, it won't be tomorrow, it might not even be next week. But we *will* get to the boys. You have my word on that."

"I'm just so worried about them, Dad. We have no way to get in touch with them, no way to find out if they're all right. I know Elliott will take care of them, but I'm their mom. They should be with me," Carly said.

"We are all worried about them, sweetie," Lauri said, "but Elliott would not let anything happen to Aaron and Cameron. If they can't be with us, that's where I would choose for them to be."

Carly nodded, wiping tears from her eyes. "I know you're both right. I just can't stop thinking about them."

Joel patted her hand as he pulled his away. "We're all thinking about them, honey, and your brother, Will. Right now, all we can do is pray they are okay while we try to figure out what we need to do to get by at the moment. Now, back to what we were talking about ..."

Just then, there was a knock at the front door. "I'll get it," Joel said, as he stood from the table. He went to the door, looked through the peephole, and saw Beth Browning, their next-door neighbor, standing on the porch, rocking back and forth on her feet in an apparent attempt to keep them warm. Joel opened the door.

"Oh, hi, Joel. I was just wondering ... um, if you could help me out. It's so cold in my house. I've never really used my fireplace, so I don't have any wood. It's just so messy, you know? Anyway, I was wondering if you could let me have some wood and maybe help me get a fire started. Wow, something smells really good in there."

Joel took his coat from the coat tree by the door and slipped his boots on. "Yeah, Beth, I can help you get one started. We don't have a lot of wood to spare, but we can get you something for right now. Give me a couple of minutes to get the wood and kindling together and I'll be right over."

Lauri walked in then with another plastic container of still warm soup. "Here, Beth, take this soup with you. Maybe it will help warm you on the inside."

Beth took the soup, wrapping both hands around the container. "Thank you so much, Lauri. How were you able to cook this? I thought you had an electric stove like me."

"We do, but we used to camp quite a bit and we still have our equipment, which includes our camp stove, so I guess we're fortunate in that respect. I'm not sure what we'll do when the propane runs out though," Lauri replied.

"Oh, I'm sure everything will be back to normal in a day or so," Beth said. "Probably just some lines down somewhere."

Joel looked at her incredulously. "Have you tried to use your cell phone, Beth?"

Beth looked at him, surprised. "Yes, there must be something wrong with it. I can't get it to power on at all. As soon as the roads clear I'll have to go to the Verizon store and let them take a look at it."

Joel then asked, "Have you tried to start your car?"

Now Beth looked confused. "No, I never drive my car when there's ice on the roads. Why?"

"I believe you'll find that your car doesn't work either," Joel replied. "Pretty much nothing does. Anyway, I'll be over with the fire supplies in less than five minutes."

"Okay, thank you both so much! See you in a few, Joel," Beth said with a smile, as she turned to go back to her house.

Joel looked at Lauri as he closed the door. "You see what I mean? Nobody gets it. Nobody can see this isn't just a power outage. When they finally figure it out — and they will — it's going to get ugly. I hope Will gets home soon. We've got to figure out how to get to Elliott's house as soon as possible. Memphis, and anywhere around it, is going to become hell on earth. I wish I'd listened to Elliott when he tried to tell me something like this could happen. I didn't want to believe it, yet here it is. And here we are, on the fringe of a city with a million people, and no way to protect ourselves."

"What are you talking about, Joel? Protect ourselves from what? From who?" Lauri said, wide-eyed. "What do you think is going to happen?"

"Nothing good, that's for sure," he remarked as he went out the back door to gather the wood to take to Beth's house.

~~~~~

Beth had been watching for Joel through the front window, so the door was opening as he walked up. He stamped his feet on the stoop and stepped into the foyer. Beth looked down at his boots, dripping slightly onto the rug in front of the door.

"Um, could you take your boots off here, Joel? I don't want the carpet to get wet."

Joel looked at her incredulously. "Well, you're going to have to deal with it, Beth, because I don't have time to worry about whether or not your floor gets a little damp from my boots I walked over here in through the snow to do you a favor. Do you want me to get you a fire started or not?"

She turned red at his admonishment. "Yes, please. Right this way." She led the way into the living room looking straight ahead. Joel followed, shaking his head in disbelief. He walked over to the fireplace and set the wood down. Kneeling down, he opened the doors and screen, and found there was no grate. Instead, there was a tiered candle holder sitting where the grate should have been. He turned to look at her.

"Well, since you don't have a grate I don't know how well it's going to burn. It won't get as much air to feed the fire."

Beth replied, "But bonfires don't have grates. Campfires don't have grates. I don't understand how this is different."

"Because those fires are built outside where the fire can get air from all directions. Inside, the fire gets air only from the front," he said, gesturing to the space in front of the fireplace, "and there won't be any movement. I'll do what I can. Do you have any newspaper?"

Beth shook her head. "No, I haven't gotten the paper in years. It's so much easier to read it online, and I don't have to worry about piles of papers that have to be bundled and hauled to the recycle center —"

Joel interrupted her. "Do you have any junk mail that's like newsprint then? Or paper plates?"

"Let me go look in the kitchen," she said as she hurried that way.

While he waited, Joel started getting his wood and supplies laid out. He had small split logs, smaller kindling size, even smaller tinder pieces, and some fatwood. He lifted the ornamental candelabra out and set it on the floor beside the fireplace. Looking around, he noticed that the living room was immaculate. Nothing was out of place, and everything matched perfectly from the drapes to the furniture to the carpet. The furniture appeared brand new and didn't look like anyone had ever used it. The living room didn't look like anyone actually lived in it. Beth came back with a few sales flyers and handed them to Joel.

"They're just a bit damp. They were in the trash can and a tea bag was put on top of them. Will they work?"

He took the papers, inspected them, and gave her a nod. "Yep, they'll do. You should probably watch how I do this in case you need to build one yourself."

She laughed. "Oh, I don't think I'll need to know that. I'm going to make an appointment to have gas logs installed as soon as the phones come back on. I can see how having some kind of actual use of a fireplace is a good thing."

Joel started to tell her that it wasn't likely that would ever happen but chose to keep it to himself. He didn't know if he should be trying to educate those around him about what their future would probably hold. He knew people like Beth most likely wouldn't make it long without the comforts they had grown accustomed to. But why did he have to be the one to break it to them? And what if he was wrong? Instead, he went back to working on the fire. He built a combination tepee log cabin in the hopes the fire would get some air between the bottom logs and it would burn for a while. He changed the subject while he worked.

"Is that new furniture in here? I was noticing how everything matches."

Beaming, Beth replied, "Oh, no, I've had it for a few years. This room is my pride and joy. That's another reason I didn't want to use the fireplace. I didn't want the smell to get into the furniture. Plus, the ashes, just too messy. I'm sure I'll have to get someone in here to clean it as soon as the power comes back on."

Joel looked at the sofa again. "You've had it for years? It looks brand new. How do you keep it looking like that, like no one ever uses it?"

"That's how. No one ever uses it," she said, as if it was the simplest thing to understand.

Joel's brow furrowed. "You never sit in here? Don't you have family or friends over sometimes?"

"Of course! But they don't sit in here. I use the den for visiting and entertaining."

"So, this room is just here and never gets used?" Joel asked, not hiding the surprise in his voice.

Now Beth was starting to take offense. "I don't see why you find that so hard to believe. Many people have formal living rooms and informal dens."

Joel shrugged. "Just seems like a waste of all the money you spent to decorate it like this and no one ever sees it."

"Everyone who comes here sees it! They walk through it to get to the den!"

Joel shook his head as he pulled the screen closed on the fireplace. "I guess I'm not fancy enough for that kind of thing. Anyway, your fire is going. You might want to check your yard, see if there's any limbs out there that might have broken off from the ice. They'll be green, but they should burn by the time this bed of coals gets built up. I gotta get back home."

Getting over her indignation, Beth became the hostess again. "Oh, okay. Thank you so much for coming over to do this, Joel. It already feels warmer in here." She was at the door and holding it open for him.

He nodded. "You're welcome. Try to stay warm, Beth." He stepped out the door onto the walkway.

"I will. Please thank Lauri again for the soup. I grabbed a spoon of it while I was waiting for you and it's delicious. You two are wonderful neighbors." She waved as she shut the door behind him.

"We'll see if you still feel that way in a couple of days," he said as he trudged back home.

Chapter 11

Cameron sat at the kitchen table, looking dejected. "This is going to last months, maybe years? That sucks, man."

Aaron nodded in agreement. "Hell yeah, it does. No television, no Internet, no cell phones, no electronics at all. I don't even know what life looks like without all that."

"It looks like a lot of work," Elliott said. "No electricity means no running water which is a lot more important than any gadgets. Even in the cities, the water's gonna stop flowing at some point. At least out here we have the well with the hand pump on it. But no more hot showers; we'll be boiling water to wash dishes and asses. And it will all have to be hauled up here from the well."

Cameron looked at the list again. "What about this one right here, Pap — chop wood every day. We've got a shed full of wood out back. Isn't it enough to get through the winter?"

"It is, but it still needs to be split into smaller pieces," Elliott replied. "The big pieces are good for banking up a fire for the night, but you need the smaller ones to get a fire started and build up a bed of coals, especially for cooking."

"Cooking? You're not going to build a fire in the oven are you, Pap?" Cameron asked, incredulously.

Elliott laughed. "No, son, but the gas in that tank outside won't last forever. In fact, we'll be lucky if it lasts the winter. When it's gone, we'll be cooking on the wood stove in there," he said, motioning to the stove in the living room. "We may even end up doing some cooking outside, especially in the summer, so we don't heat up the house."

"It's unreal to think about being here for months, planning how we're going to cook next summer. I'm guessing you know how to do all that, Pap," Aaron commented. "You know, cooking on the wood stove, over a campfire, that kind of stuff."

"Lord, yes, that's how I was raised," Elliott said. "My granny's house was basically two rooms: the living room and kitchen were one big room. She cooked over the fire in the fireplace. My mama had a wood-burning cook stove in her kitchen and a wood-burning stove in the living room. I helped cook on all of them."

"Well, at least we won't starve," Cameron said. "How long will the food here last? Oh man! No more pizzas, hamburgers, tacos ... none of the things a growing boy needs to exist!"

"No, we won't starve, Cam, but, yeah, we will be eating different than you're used to, I'm guessing," Elliott replied. "I reckon for just the three of us, if you throw in some hunting, we could go four, maybe six months, with the food here; but we're gonna need to do something about the meat in the freezer before it warms up again. When your mom and grandparents get here, we'll be cooking for twice as many people, so that will cut the length of time the food will last in half. What we have will get us through to the spring, and then it will be planting time. Hey! That reminds me — the tractor! Maybe it still runs. In fact, I bet it will, since it's about seventy years old. Let's go check."

Pulling on their coats, the three of them walked out the back door to the barn. The snow seemed to be tapering off and it looked like the sun was trying to come through the dense clouds. Once inside, Elliott climbed on the old Ford 9N tractor. He adjusted the gear shift to neutral and opened the throttle about halfway. He turned the key, and after just a moment the tractor fired up.

"Hot dog! Now we're talking!" Elliott exclaimed, as the boys exchanged a high-five. "I feel better already knowing we have a vehicle that works, such as it is." He let it run for a minute, then turned the key off and placed it in his coat

93

pocket. "Don't reckon I'll be leaving the key in it anymore. If somebody comes to steal her, I'm sure not gonna make it easy for them. Speaking of stealing, we might ought to go ahead and get you boys some gun training in. The world's probably gonna get a whole lot meaner real soon. Plus, we need everybody who can to help with the hunting … and other things."

Cameron seemed confused. "What other things, Pap?"

Elliott looked at his grandson, sadness apparent on his face. "If this lasts for a while, and it probably will, people are going to run out of food because there won't be any more deliveries to Kroger. The longer they go without food, the more desperate they're going to get. They'll start breaking into people's houses and stealing whatever they can find. Hungry people ain't nice. In fact, they're dangerous and we need to be ready for that."

"Ready how, exactly?" Aaron asked.

"To do whatever we have to do to protect what's ours," Elliott replied resolutely. "If we let somebody take what we have, we'll be right there with them trying to get supplies from somewhere. We have food, not enough to last forever, but enough to get us through until we can grow more. Plus, when the rest of them get out here, we'll need every bit of it to feed us all. We have to keep what we have. The only way I know to make sure no one takes it is to shoot them if they try."

"What? You want us to shoot people?" The shock in Aaron's tone was hard to miss.

"Hell no! I don't want anybody to shoot anybody," Elliott replied. "But if anybody tries to take our stuff, I won't hesitate to make sure they don't."

"Pap, I think you're worried about something that isn't going to happen," Cameron said. "I don't think people will act like that. They'll probably just come to the door, knock, and ask if we have anything to spare."

94

"Oh, they will, at first — ask, that is. What do you think they'll do when we say no? Especially when they see that we ain't starving. They'll be back, and they won't be nice, at all." Elliott sighed. "But we're not gonna worry about that right now. First thing we're going to do is teach you boys how to clean a gun."

"I thought we were going to shoot, not clean," Cameron complained.

Elliott chuckled. "You're going to learn all of it, Cam, starting with the cleaning. Besides, we can do that part inside where it's warm."

"I'm all for that," Aaron commented. "Cleaning inside sounds real good to me right now."

"My feelings exactly," Elliott replied as he headed for the house.

An hour later, the boys were enjoying the *chore* so much they asked for more guns to clean. Elliott smiled and brought out all he had. He showed them how to break each one down, what and where to clean, and how to put them back together. He looked into the living room where his small Christmas tree stood in the corner. There were packages with both boys' names on them, along with Carly, Joel, and Lauri. He made a decision and went to the tree, pulling two long packages from behind it and bringing them to the kitchen. Both boys saw the brightly wrapped packages he held and looked at him surprised.

"Hey, Pap, what ya got there?" Cameron asked excitedly. "Is it for me ... er, us?"

Elliott grinned. "This is part of your Christmas, but with what's going on, I think I need to go ahead and give them to you now. Merry Christmas, boys!" He handed each one of them a package.

With huge smiles, they tore into the presents. Tearing the paper away revealed a brand-new rifle for each boy.

Elliott had decided he would give them each one of his pistols, but he wanted them to have a firearm no one else had owned as well, and in the current situation two more rifles might very well be needed. For Aaron, he had chosen a Remington model 783, chambered in .308. Cameron's was also a .308, but his was a Savage Arms AXIS. Both were bolt action, and both had scopes. The boys were speechless as they looked at the brand-new guns. Finally, Aaron found his voice.

"Pap! Oh my God! This is *the* coolest gift I think I've ever gotten. Thank you, thank you *so* much. It's just awesome!" He was holding the gun with the butt on his leg and the barrel pointed at the ceiling, his hand on the stock, admiring the rifle. Cameron, on the other hand, was tracking his around the room, peering through the scope with one eye closed, finger on the trigger.

"Yeah, Pap! This is the bomb! When can we shoot it?"

"When you learn how to respect it for one thing. Quit pointing that thing around and get your damn finger off the trigger *now*!" Elliott barked at his grandson. Cameron immediately moved his finger and laid the rifle on the table. "Good Lord, son, what if it had been loaded and you accidentally pulled the trigger?"

Chastised, Cameron said quietly, "Sorry, but you wouldn't have given me a loaded rifle for a present, Pap. Would you?"

Elliott shook his head. "No, but the first rule of owning or handling a firearm is to treat all guns as if they're loaded, even if you know they aren't. I'm mad at myself for waiting this long to teach you boys about guns. That's why I wanted you this week. Now, with what's happened, the timing couldn't have been better. I know you're worried about your mom; I am, too. But I'm so glad you're here instead of there where she is. If that makes me selfish, so be it. You boys are about the only family I have left. Here, I can try to keep you safe. There, who knows what's going to happen in a few days."

Elliott paused. They weren't sure, but he seemed to be trying to compose himself before he went on. Neither of the boys said anything. Taking a deep breath, he continued.

"I know this doesn't seem real to you boys. Hell, it taxes my brain thinking about how things are going to be now. On top of everything else, if this was a nuke, somebody had to have done it on purpose. Don't know how, don't know why, and we may not know anything for a while. Honestly, there ain't much we can do about it anyway. If we're under attack, they'll show up sooner or later. We'll deal with that then. Right now, we just need to get through today, then tomorrow, then the next day. Let's start with you two getting to know your new rifles."

Chapter 12

Longworth House Office Building, Office of Phil Roman, Speaker of the House

Phil Roman sat at his large ornate desk staring at nothing. He had sent word to the vice-president that he needed to speak with him immediately. As yet, he had not heard back from him. Knowing that the VP would do exactly what Olstein told him to was no consolation. The man second in the line of succession to the White House was at a loss as to how to proceed. A knock on his door brought him out of the trance-like state he was in.

"Come in," he called out halfheartedly. The door opened, and General Charles Everley entered. Roman closed his eyes for a moment, gave a brief nod, and indicated the chair on the other side of his desk. "General. Can't say I'm surprised. Have a seat."

Everley closed the door behind him and sat in the chair Roman had indicated. Taking a deep breath, he began. "Mr. Speaker —"

Roman interrupted him. "Oh, I think at this point, we can dispense with the formalities, Charles."

"Okay, Phil," Everley replied as he unbuttoned his dress jacket. "I'm sure you know why I'm here."

Roman inclined his head to the side. "Probably, but why don't you spell it out for me anyway."

"What the president is proposing is treason. He is declaring war on millions of Americans for no other reason than that they have things he wants to give to others or, in the case of the guns, doesn't want them to have so they have the ability to fight back when his jackboots try to take their supplies. He is planning to all but abandon the rural communities to fend for themselves, after he takes everything they could use to do that. Are we just going to sit on our asses and let this happen?" Everley's voice rose an octave with each sentence until he was almost shouting.

Roman patted the air indicating that Everley keep it down. "Easy, Charles. If your face gets any redder, I think I might be able to light a cigarette off it — that is, if I still smoked. After this morning, I've contemplated taking up the habit again." Roman sighed and went on. "To be perfectly honest, I'm not really sure what our next move should be. I've sent a runner to the vice-president's residence asking for a meeting. That was right after the meeting with the president, which I was surprised that he didn't attend. I haven't gotten word that he is even still in Washington. He may have already left for the holiday. Any action on our part has to include him. I don't have a lot of faith that he will cooperate though."

Everley spluttered, "He's Olstein's puppet! He'll never be a part of any action against him. That is what we're talking about here, right? Removing him from office?"

"If we follow the Constitution, it's impossible to impeach him. Congress is in recess. Most of the members are already home for the holidays. With the situation the way it is, they probably won't be back here for quite a while. There's no way to initiate the proceedings." Roman paused, then went on. "However, the president is certainly not following the Constitution, as he does not have the power to seize personal assets of citizens without warrants and probable cause. He absolutely does not have the power to repeal the Second Amendment. I'm not comfortable with the alternatives in any choice."

"What about what he said … that he won't step down for Tanner? He can't do that, can he?" Everley asked.

"No, and that may be our saving grace. Mr. Tanner is in New York City, which is not that far. We should be able to get him here, and I think we need to make that a priority. Do you have someone you could task with that assignment?"

Everley nodded. "I'll get someone on it ASAP. That's all we need, right? Him to be here, to assume control on January 20th?"

Roman hesitated. "Well, there's a small problem, and I'm not sure how important it is or may become."

"What problem?"

"Congress is supposed to meet on January 6th to confirm the electoral college votes. That's the final step that makes the election official. I doubt that's going to happen," Roman said.

Everley's eyes grew wide. "Can he use that to his advantage? If he doesn't step down, it's effectively a coup. On top of everything else we have going on in this country, we can't let that happen."

"Agreed, and that's why I want to get President-elect Tanner here immediately. It will be much harder for Olstein to hold power with his successor literally waiting in the wings."

"All right, let me get to work on that right now." Everley stood, buttoned and tugged down the bottom of his jacket, and reached a hand across the desk toward the congressman.

Roman stood as well and shook the general's hand. "And, Charles? I'm sure I don't need to say it but I'm going to anyway. We need to keep this very quiet. Only the absolute minimum number of people should know what we're trying to accomplish. I wouldn't venture a guess as to what lengths Olstein will take to hold onto the power he now has — albeit not nearly as much as he thinks he has —

but people's lives could be in danger, including yours and mine. We should take nothing for granted at this point."

Everley gave him a solemn nod. "Agreed. For now, you, me, and the man I'll be sending to New York are the only ones who will know about this meeting or the decisions we've made from it. I think we have a solid start to a good plan."

"I do, too," Roman said with a small smile. "I just hope we can keep him from completely destroying the Constitution and the country — or what's left of it after all this — before we can get it implemented."

"Your oath had the same line in it that mine did — to support and defend the Constitution from all enemies foreign and domestic. We are seeing firsthand why they put that last part in. I'll be in touch, Phil." Everley turned and went out the door.

Roman replied softly to the closing door, "Thank God for the founding fathers' wisdom and foresight."

~~~~~~

The Pentagon, Office of General Charles Everley, Chief of Staff of the Army

Major Damon Sorley had been General Everley's aide since he'd lost a part of his thigh muscle to an IED in Afghanistan three years before. Sitting at a desk wasn't his idea of Army life, but Damon figured somebody had to push the papers; and since his injury put him at less than one hundred percent, taking him out of the fight, he might as well take the post when it was offered. The rigorous physical therapy he had gone through for almost a year had given him the use of the leg again, but he would walk with a limp for the rest of his life. When he woke up that morning and found nothing electrical working, he had quickly donned a uniform and walked the mile to the Pentagon from his apartment in the Crystal Towers. He was glad he had chosen civilian housing over the base at Ft. Belvoir. He probably couldn't have made it from there — at least, not nearly as fast. He was past due to rotate out to another post, since aides usually only stayed with a senior officer for two years, but Everley had the juice to keep him where he was. Damon wasn't unhappy about it. He liked the general, liked that he was a no bullshit kind of guy, and that he didn't get caught up in all the political crap that others did, especially in DC.

Everley returned from his meeting with Phil Roman and motioned to Damon to follow him. Damon grabbed a pad and paper and went into the general's office. As he removed his coat, Everley said, "Have a seat, Damon." Damon sat in the chair across from Everley's. Charles hung his coat on a hook then sat at his desk. To Damon, he looked like he hadn't slept in three days.

"Can I get you some coffee, Sir? You look like you could use it," Damon said, starting to rise.

Everley shook his head. "Not right now. I need to talk to you about something, and it can't leave this room."

Damon sat up a bit straighter. "Of course, General. Is everything okay?"

"No, everything most certainly is not okay, Major." Charles proceeded to tell Damon everything that had transpired that morning up to that point. Damon listened without comment until Everley paused after the part about the president's plans. Seeing an opening, he spoke up.

"He can't do that, can he, Sir? Repeal the Second Amendment? Stay in office when his term is up? I mean, this is America, for Christ's sake, not some socialist country." Damon didn't attempt to hide the shock in his voice. "Seriously, this is insane! We have to do something!"

Everley let a small smile show on his face. "I was hoping you'd feel that way, Damon." He continued his narrative with the meeting with Roman and what they had discussed. "So, now that you know, I need to ask a favor of you."

"Of course, I'll go to New York and find Mr. Tanner," Damon said before Charles could put the request into words. "All I need is a working vehicle and thirty minutes to get home and pack a bag. Depending on how jammed up the roads are, I can be there before dark."

Charles nodded. "Good. I'll have a Humvee waiting out front when you leave. Get me the motor pool on the line."

Damon hesitated. "Uh, we don't have phones, Sir."

"Dammit! Fine, I'll walk you down to the motor pool."

Damon stood. "Yes, Sir. Is there anything else?"

"Yes, draw up a letter from me to whom it may concern giving you access to any facility you need, military or civilian. Olstein is enacting martial law and I don't want you caught up in any of that bullshit. You'll have to handwrite it so make it quick. And Major?"

Damon had turned to head for the door but stopped at the utterance of his title. "Sir?"

"I'm serious about no one knowing why you're going to New York. If Olstein finds out, I'm sure he'll try to stop you."

Solemnly, Damon replied, "I understand, Sir. Don't worry. I've got this."

He went to his desk and pulled a blank piece of paper from the printer. Staring at it, he began to compose the message in his head beforehand. Once he had a good idea of what it needed to say, he started to write.

From the office of General Charles Everley, Chief of Staff of the Army

To Whom It May Concern:

The bearer of this missive, Major Damon Sorley, has unlimited authority to enter any facility, military or civilian, in pursuit of his assigned mission. He is not at liberty to share the details of this mission but know that it is of the utmost importance and vital to national security, so it is imperative that he be allowed to continue unfettered to complete said mission. Any attempt to detain him shall be met with the full force of this office and dealt with most harshly.

Any questions should be directed to my office.

Sincerely,

General Charles Everley

Chief of Staff of the Army

Short but sweet, that's how the general liked his memos. Damon had never drafted one without a template from the server to start with, and he had never written one for this precise situation before, but he thought this would suffice. He picked it up, walked to the general's door, and knocked.

"Come in, Major," Charles called out.

He walked in and without saying anything laid the memo on the general's desk. Everley looked it over, smiled, and signed it with a flourish. "Perfect. Exactly what I wanted to say but much more professionally than I would have said it. Now, let's go get you a ride. The sooner you get on your way, the sooner you can get back here, hopefully with someone who can do something to stop this insanity."

True to his word, thirty minutes later Damon was on his way to New York. He had packed another uniform and two sets of civilian clothes in his small duffel bag and picked up his service-issued Sig P320 and personal side arm, a Beretta 92FS, both chambered in nine-millimeter. The Beretta was identical to his previous service pistol, the M9, and he was very comfortable with it. He also had an AK wrapped in a large sweatshirt and 500 rounds of ammo for the guns in his duffel. The Sig was in a holster at his side, the Beretta under the seat. He had also grabbed a bag of chips, a couple of apples, and a six-pack of water from his place. He hoped this early in the event he could get there and back without any trouble, but he wasn't taking any chances, thus the guns. With no other cars moving on the streets, outside of the occasional military vehicle, he was through the district in minutes. Getting on I-95, he headed north.

Chapter 13

The closer they got to the first real exit of any kind, the fewer people Will and Amanda found still with their vehicles. Apparently, seeing signs on the ramp for food, gas, and lodging had prompted the occupants of the now empty cars and trucks to attempt to make it to shelter, or at least some semblance of services. They passed a couple of cars whose inhabitants appeared to be asleep. At least, that's what Will was hoping they were doing. He wasn't entirely sure how long it would take a person to freeze to death in a car, but with temperatures in the upper twenties and most people without proper clothing, or even blankets, he wouldn't have been surprised to find out some of those caught on the road had already died. Having not worn a watch for many years, because his phone told him the time when he needed to know, he had no idea what time it was. He was guessing it was about noon, which would put these people out in the elements with no protection or way to stay warm for about eight hours.

Amanda seemed to be thinking along the same lines. She peered into the driver's window of a small sedan where a senior-aged woman appeared to be sleeping with her head against the window of the door. She turned to Will and asked quietly, "Should we check on her?"

Will took in the woman's appearance. She looked quite pale, almost blue. He shook his head as he continued down the road. "There's nothing we can do for her either way, Amanda. If she's just sleeping, we can't make her any more comfortable or bring her with us. If she's gone, she's gone. We're almost to the ramp. We're about five miles from my mom and dad. Let's just keep moving."

Dejectedly, Amanda fell into step beside Will. They walked along in silence, both apparently lost in their own thoughts. As they got to the bottom of the ramp, Will stopped and turned to her. "You do know that I hate not being able to help anyone as much as you do, right? I'm pretty sure that woman was dead. She wasn't dressed for this weather. She may have had a heart condition or even a heart attack. Knowing for sure wasn't going to help her or us. It totally sucks, but I don't know what else to do except to keep going until I get home. Are you cool with that?"

She hesitated a moment, long enough for Will to second-guess himself on saying anything to her about the situation. Then, with a slight inclination of her head, she replied, "I get it, Will. I hate it, but I get it. You're right — there probably wasn't anything we could do for her. I just feel so selfish, you know? I didn't plan for this either, but, luckily, I have what I need to get somewhere safe ... well, safer than my car on a lonely stretch of highway. She didn't have anything, barely a winter coat. How does that saying go? There but for the grace of God, go I ..."

Will nodded. "Yep, I've been thinking along those lines myself. This winter storm made me pack differently than I normally would for a trip home. Any other time, I wouldn't have had these boots, extra layers of clothing, any of those things. And if it had happened an hour earlier, the chance of me making it home would've been a whole lot less. I really feel like I'm supposed to get there, and honestly that's all I can think about right now."

With a small smile, Amanda replied, "Then let's get there."

Will returned her smile and headed up the ramp.

Had he been driving, Will would not have gotten off the interstate on the Highway 64 exit. There was so much traffic in that area that it actually took him longer to get to his parents' house from there than going on down to Appling Road. On foot, however, he would cut a few miles off of his journey by taking the earlier exit. At least, that's what he hoped.

Lauri and Joel lived on Olive Street, in an area of Bartlett that hadn't yet been gobbled up by developers. Older homes with large yards and houses not on top of each other comprised their neighborhood. There was a small park just down the street, but it was across 4th Avenue. The Chambers lived on the south side of 4th where Olive Street ended. Will would have to travel Highway 64 until he got to Appling Road, which he would take north to the area his parents and sister lived in. Carly lived a couple of miles further on Pecanhill Drive. He still had a way to go, but just being off the interstate made him feel like he was making progress.

He was in no way prepared for the sight that greeted them when they got on Stage Road, otherwise known as Highway 64. A busy area in the best situation, there were people everywhere, except they were all on foot. They were in various stages of dress, from pajamas with a winter coat over them, to full-on heavy hunting gear. His best guess as to the cause was the Walmart located just past the exit. As they approached the Walmart parking lot, the sounds of angry, impatient people grew louder, along with the sound of heavy objects hitting glass. He took Amanda by the arm and quickly ushered her across the street.

"What? What is it?" she asked anxiously.

"Just trying to avoid what is fast approaching an ugly situation over there," Will said, indicating the large store across the street from them now.

Amanda looked over to see what Will was referring to. "Oh, wow! That *is* getting ugly. What's going on?"

Will continued on, picking up the pace a bit. "My guess is desperate people trying to get things with credit cards that don't work and checks that will not be accepted because they can't be verified. Most people don't carry cash, just like you. Not only that, the managers probably won't let people in the store because they can't watch everybody — no security cameras now. Unfortunately, the mob will surely win and somebody's going to get hurt. Let's make sure it isn't us."

At the sound of multiple voices raised in triumph, they stopped for a moment and looked across the street. The glass front of the store had finally shattered. People were streaming in, with no regard for anyone around them. They watched in shock as men, women, and children were trampled in the mad rush of the mob to enter the store.

"Oh my God! Did you see that?" Amanda exclaimed.

Taking her arm again, facing forward, Will continued down the sidewalk. "Yes, that's what I was afraid of. Just keep moving. We need to get out of here, fast."

They weren't out of the woods though. Along with multiple restaurants and car dealerships, entrances to Wolfchase Galleria were there as well. Once they had passed Walmart, Will took them back across the street, away from Wolfchase, which had its own share of people around the outside of it, voices raised in protest of the locked doors. Now on the same side of the street as Lowe's, raised voices seemed to be coming at them from all directions. The home improvement store would've been a likely choice for things such as generators to power homes suddenly without power. Yet, it would be the same scenario there as anywhere else. In the modern world, everything was digital, including currency. People with bank accounts of four and five figures became indignant when they had no access to it. Worst of all, large chain stores had no protocol for how to operate without electricity.

"We're what, eight, ten hours into this? Can you imagine what this area is going to be like by nightfall if this goes on?" Amanda commented, awestruck at the way the people were acting.

"Unfortunately, yes, I can, and we don't want to be anywhere near this place then." Will picked up the pace yet again, especially as they approached Target, which was a very similar scene to what had happened at Walmart, except the mob had already broken through the doors and people were running out with baskets of goods, many of which would not work now. Large TVs, coffee makers, and microwaves were pointless, but the mob didn't get that yet. Once they got past the store, they didn't have far to go to reach Appling Road. Except they didn't quite make it without being accosted.

"Hey, you! Chick with the big backpack! Where'd you get that?" a man yelled at them from across the street.

Will said under his breath, "Just ignore him. Keep walking."

Amanda did as he said and continued on without replying to the man. However, the stranger would not be so easily dismissed.

"Hey! I'm talking to you!" the man said as he started across the street toward them.

The visions of people attacking others vivid in his memory, Will stepped in front of Amanda, putting himself between her and the stranger. "We don't want any trouble. We're just trying to get home."

"Then answer my damn question — where'd you get the big backpack?" The stranger replied belligerently.

Amanda started to reply, but Will interrupted her. "We had these supplies with us when we got stranded on the interstate. We didn't *get* them anywhere. We already had them. We've been walking a long time and we just want to get home. We're going to be on our way now."

The stranger stopped in the middle of the street, eyeing both of them. Will took the opportunity to turn to Amanda and, with a brief indication of his head, direct her to continue down the street.

Once they were out of earshot of the stranger, who was still staring at them from the middle of the road, Amanda asked, "What was that all about? You cut me off and didn't let me speak for myself. I'm fully capable of handling a situation like that on my own."

He knew this was coming. How was he going to explain to her the dangers they would be facing in the next days, weeks, months, probably longer, if his visions were coming true? How could he make her understand how perilous their lives would become very soon without telling her how he knew that? He still wasn't ready to tell her about that part of himself, not yet anyway. Instead, he tried to make light of it.

"I'm sorry, I'm sure you can take care of yourself. I guess it's just the Southern gentleman ingrained in me to protect the damsel in distress," he replied sheepishly, still not ready to share his gift, or curse, depending on how you looked at it, with her.

She smirked at him. "Oh, I see how it is now. I'm a damsel in distress and you're here to save me."

He grinned at her and said, "Maybe more like protect you from yourself. Seriously though, that could've gone bad fast and just the wrong word or tone could have set him off. We should try really hard not to interact with anybody unless we absolutely have to. These people are going to get more and more worked up as the day goes on. Thankfully, we don't have a lot more retail real estate to deal with before we get to the burbs. So, are you done being mad at me?"

"I guess I'll have to be," she said with a make-believe heavy sigh.

"Thank you, because we're just two or three miles from my parents' house. We should be there in an hour, two tops, depending on how clogged the roads are."

"What difference will that make? We'll be on the sidewalk," Amanda replied.

"Not while we're going down Appling Road we won't. That's mostly industrial property up through there, no need for sidewalks. Add to that it's Sunday morning, so there probably hasn't been a lot of traffic on it either. I expect the road to be ice. We'll have to take our time and be careful," Will said. "The upside is there shouldn't be a lot of people out and about on that section, at least not until we get up by the police department and Kroger on Summer Avenue, which will probably be a nightmare, too. We'll worry about that one when we get there. Let's get going."

Performing a pretend curtsy with a pretend dress, Amanda said, "Lead the way, Southern gentleman."

Will chuckled as he headed down the sidewalk. "Smart ass."

Chapter 14

Joel stamped his feet on the front porch trying to knock as much snow off as he could before he went into the house. He walked in and hung his coat on the knob of the closet door in the entryway. He had a feeling he would be needing it quite a bit as the day went on, so he didn't bother to hang it up inside. As he walked into the living room, he saw Carly sitting by the fire drying her hair. "How did your hair get wet?" he asked, confused.

"Oh, I didn't get to take a shower this morning at my house, so I just grabbed one here," she replied. "I felt pretty grungy from riding in that trailer. I feel much better now."

Voice full of frustration, Joel barked, "You do realize that the water in that tank is a precious commodity now, right?"

Lauri came in from the kitchen at the sound of her husband's raised voice. She took in her daughter's chastened face and her husband's red one. "What's wrong?"

"Your daughter just helped herself to the last hot shower any of us will likely have for a while," Joel said. "Probably half of the forty gallons of water in the tank, too."

Carly looked crestfallen. "I'm sorry, Dad, I didn't think …"

"No, you didn't think. Our water heater is electric. Our stove is electric. Everything in this place is electric except for that wood-burning fireplace you're sitting in front of. I don't know how else to explain this to you so that you will understand. Unless I'm wrong about what this is, everything is going to stop working, including the water. We need to save as much as we can until your brother gets here and we decide what we're going to do."

"What do you mean decide what we're going to do? I thought we were going to Elliott's, where the boys are." Carly looked at her father stubbornly. "If that's not your plan, Dad, let me know now because it *is* mine. I *have* to get to my sons. If you're not going, I'll figure out a way to get there by myself. I'm sure I can get Will to go with me."

Joel shook his head and replied, "That is *not* what I meant. Of course, we're going to try to get to Aaron and Cameron. I just haven't figured out how yet. And we're not doing anything until your brother has a chance to get home. Agreed?"

Lips pressed together tightly for moment, Carly gave her father a curt nod. "Agreed. And I am sorry about the shower. I'm still having a hard time wrapping my brain around the fact that this isn't just a power outage. I mean, are you absolutely sure that's not what this is, Dad?"

"I'm absolutely sure. The cars and the phones are the clincher. A power outage wouldn't affect those."

Carly closed her eyes and threw her head back. "You're right, you're right, I know you're right, but I just don't want to believe it. I mean, how — how can everything not work? Don't answer that. I know, because you told me. My mind is just not processing it." She growled in frustration as she got up from the floor. "I'm going to go hang this towel in the bathroom, then I'm going to dig one of those beers out of the cooler on the patio. You guys in?"

Both of her parents replied with a yes. When Carly had left the room, Lauri spoke softly to her husband. "Was that really necessary, Joel? Did you have to be that rough with her? This is hard on all of us. I'm right there with her. I keep trying to turn on light switches and check my phone to see what time it is."

Joel sighed. "I didn't mean to be that harsh. I'm frustrated, too. But I'm also worried about a lot of things. I'm worried about Will, wondering where he is, if he's all right. I'm worried about using the generator, because there's no way to keep the neighbors from hearing it running. I'm worried about the neighbors. They're clueless now, but in a few days, maybe as early as tomorrow, it's going to start sinking in that this isn't just a power outage. Most of them won't understand what it is but that won't lessen their fear. It will probably make it worse because we fear the unknown much more than the known. I'm sure some of them will adapt. I'm just as sure some of them won't, probably the majority of them, and that they won't make it. I don't want us to be the ones who don't make it. We're barely better off than most of the others around here, and that's only because we have a generator, chickens, and your canned vegetables. What we don't have is a way to protect those things or ourselves, like I said before."

"Protect them? From what, or whom?" Lauri asked.

"Protect what? What are you guys talking about?" Carly asked as she walked back into the room.

"Our supplies, honey," Lauri answered. "Your dad thinks they need protection."

Carly handed out the beers. "From what?"

"Like mother, like daughter," Joel said with a shake of his head as he twisted the cap off the bottle. Becoming serious again, he took a swig then went on. "We need to protect them from hungry, desperate people. I don't know how long we're going to be here, because I don't know how long it will take us to find a way to get to Elliott and the boys. I want to make sure we have enough food and water to get us through until we get out there."

"Surely there's enough, Joel. The pantry is full," Lauri replied.

"What about water? I'm not talking about just for drinking or cooking. What about washing? And one I'm sure no one has thought of … what about flushing the toilets? When the water stops flowing from the faucets, it will stop going to the toilets as well."

Lauri and Carly were silent as they took in what Joel had said. When they didn't comment, he went on. "It will take about one to two gallons of water to flush the toilet. That's two less gallons of drinking water. I've actually been thinking about going out and scooping up as much of the snow on the ground as I can, then pulling the rain barrels out of the shed and filling them up with snow. I always drain them and put them up in the fall after the gardens are done. I think we may have to take a chance on them freezing to try to capture any moisture we can for that one thing. At least we won't cut into our drinking water as fast if we have other options."

"I'll help you get the snow, Dad," Carly offered. "I don't guess I ever really thought about how much we depend on electricity and the technology it provides before now. It's always been there, you know? I absolutely never considered it could just disappear. It's been hours, you've told me how it is now, how it's going to be, and I still can't make myself believe it. It just doesn't seem real."

Joel nodded. "I know, but the reality is it *is* real. Most people out there are like you, Carly. They've never known a world without electricity. A lot of them have never known one without technology. They are going to have no idea how to deal with this. And when they finally figure it out — when they finally realize no one's coming to help them — they're going to have to try to find food and water. If they don't, they'll die. They'll go door to door looking for someone to help them, to tell them what to do, how to deal with this impossible situation. They'll be scared and probably desperate, if they've been out of food for a few days. The majority of people in this country today have never gone hungry. They have no idea what that's like. Unfortunately, a lot of them are about to find out."

116

He paused, looking preoccupied, like his thoughts were a million miles away. Thoughts of what the days ahead would bring for his family and those around them seemed to weigh heavy on his mind. Lauri went over to him and wrapped her arms around him. He returned the hug. After a moment, she leaned back and looked up at her husband. With a look of resolve, she said, "Tell us what we need to do, Joel. How can we help?"

His eyes cleared, and he replied, "I guess we can start by gathering up snow out back. We're absolutely in a holding pattern until Will gets home. After that, well, we'll see how things go here in the neighborhood. I'm not making any promises about what we'll do yet. I'm pretty sure it's going to get ugly, and I don't think it will take long to get there. And we still need to figure out how to get to Elliott and the boys. Right now, let's go gather some frozen water."

By the time they had filled the three fifty-gallon rain barrels with as much snow as they could, the sun was heading past the crest of the southern sky. At least, that's where it seemed to be. The thick cloud cover had it obscured from sight. There was still a light snow falling and the temperature had not reached thirty degrees. Joel knew that when the snow melted, possibly starting the next day, they would have little water left to show for it. He removed the downspouts from a couple of spots on the back side of the house and positioned the barrels underneath them. While it wasn't the closed off process he used during the spring and summer to gather every drop of rain water for the garden, it would at least catch a portion of the melting snow and ice from the roof.

When they came back inside, they were huddled around the fireplace warming their hands when there was another knock on the door. Joel looked out the front window, turned back to the women and said, "Jack Duncan. He lives across the street from Beth," he added for Carly's benefit. He opened the door, saying, "Hey, Jack. What's up?"

"Hey, Joel. Yeah, so, I saw smoke coming out of Beth's chimney — first time ever, by the way — and I went over and asked her where she got the wood. She said you hooked her up, and I was wondering if you had any more you could spare."

Joel looked at the man in wonder. "You have a fireplace and no wood?"

Jack chuckled. "I know, right? Margie thought it was messy and didn't want the smell to get into the furniture. We were planning to convert to gas logs this year, so we'd get at least some use out of it. As of this morning, Margie has decided she can deal with the mess and will worry about the smell later when she isn't freezing. Seriously though, I'm more worried about the kids. We've got everybody bundled up in thick clothes, winter coats, blankets, you name it, but it just isn't enough. Can you help us out?"

At the mention of children, Joel's resolve melted slightly, and he said, "I can only spare a few pieces of seasoned wood, but that'll be enough to get a fire going if you're willing to cut one of your trees to use after that. I've got a chainsaw you can borrow if you know how to use it. If you don't, I can show you."

Jack's brow furrowed. "Hmm. Wow. Do you really think that's necessary?"

Growing weary of his neighbors' shortsightedness, Joel replied sharply, "I do. What do you think caused this, Jack? The power, electronics, the cars … and please don't say ice on the lines."

"No, I know power lines down wouldn't have anything to do with the cars and the phones, but I don't know what did cause it. Do you?" Jack asked.

118

"Yes, I have an idea, and it's not something that's going to be fixed anytime soon. You need to start trying to figure out how you're going to keep your family warm and fed. But I'm not talking about today, this week, or even this month. This will take months, possibly years to come back from. You've got a day or two at the most to get your hands on whatever supplies you can. I hope you have some cash because plastic is useless right now and the stores probably won't take checks. It's only about a half of a mile to the Dollar Tree, and that's where I'd go first if I were you. I'm sure Kroger is a madhouse right now." Joel stopped for a moment to catch his breath. Jack took the opportunity to speak up.

"Wait, what? What are you saying, Joel? What do you think has happened?" Jack's voice had taken on a worried tone.

Joel looked his neighbor in the eye and calmly replied, "I think we've been hit with an EMP, and I think it's gonna be a long time before we see normal again."

After inviting Jack inside, Joel gave him a brief rundown of what he knew about EMPs and what they could do to the country's electrical grid. The more information Joel shared, the paler Jack became, until they were afraid he might pass out. Joel led him to the sofa to sit down and Lauri brought him a cup of coffee. Seeing their beer bottles on the coffee table, he said, "I'll take one of those if you have one to spare. I think I need something to settle my nerves instead of caffeine."

"Coming right up," Carly said, as she jumped up and headed for the cooler on the patio. She handed him the ice-cold bottle, then picked up her own. Holding it aloft, she said loudly, "Let's take a moment to mourn the loss of our beloved electricity. Life is about to suck on a grand scale." She tipped the bottle up and drained its contents.

119

Lauri called out, "Carly!" as Joel chuckled at her comments. Jack seemed to come out of his state somewhat at Carly's remarks.

"I completely agree, Carly," Jack said forlornly. "Everything in our house — for that matter, our lives — relies on electricity. You're telling me nothing is going to work for a long time. I don't know what we're going to do, not long-term anyway. We don't have any family close. I've never hunted or fished. Hell, I don't even own any guns. I'm a computer tech, which is an absolutely worthless skill set in this scenario. I don't know what to do, what my next step is."

Joel patted the man on the shoulder. "I'll tell you what I'd do. I'd go home, get a fire started, then sit down with Margie and explain to her what's happened. Then, make that walk to the Dollar Tree. See if you can get any supplies with the cash you have. If you can, great, but if you can't or it looks dangerous, just come back home. It's going to get bad out there, if it hasn't already. You don't want to be around that, not when you have a family counting on you to take care of them.

"Start cooking and eating the food in your refrigerator. That will go bad first. Put things like milk and eggs in coolers and set them outside in your backyard. They'll keep in these temps at least for the next couple of days. Next, work on the things in the freezer. As long as you keep it closed you may have a couple of days, depending on how full it is. Don't worry about making meals that contain the five food groups. Cook what's going to go bad over the next few days if you don't eat it. Save the canned goods and pasta for last.

"Clean your tubs with bleach and fill them with water. You're going to need every drop. That small lake at the end of the road has fish, so when it warms up in a couple of days, I'll take you down there and show you how to catch fish and how to clean them. When the water you have runs out, and it will, you can bring water back from the lake. Strain it through a coffee filter or paper towel and boil it before you drink it or use it for cooking. That should be enough to either get you started or make your head explode. Maybe both."

Jack stood up, drained his beer, and handed the bottle to Joel. "I'm gonna go with both. Thank you, Joel. I appreciate the offer of the help, and I'll definitely take you up on it. And I would like to borrow that chainsaw. Looks like I'm gonna be real busy real fast."

Joel nodded, and replied, "We all are if we want to make it through this."

Chapter 15

Elliott spent over an hour with the boys going over the rifles from one end to the other. He made sure they knew how to load and unload their own and each other's rifles, where the safety was and how to engage it, and how to chamber a round. He drilled into them the importance of knowing where the gun was pointed, what it was pointed at, and what was beyond their target. He watched them intently, making sure they were always paying attention to what they were doing and how they were doing it. When he was confident they understood the mechanics, he announced, "Okay, I think you boys are ready to do a little shooting. Lay those rifles on the table and get your coats."

The boys did as they were told. After donning their coats, they started back towards the table to get their guns. Elliott stopped them.

"No, just leave those there. You won't be needing them right now," he said.

"Huh? How are we gonna shoot if we don't take our guns?" Cameron asked, then grinned, saying, "Our guns. How cool does that sound?" Aaron nodded in agreement with a big smile on his face.

"I said we were gonna do some shooting. I didn't say we were going to shoot those guns. You need to start out small and work your way up." Elliott walked over to the table and picked up a Ruger 10/22. "We'll start with this one. Come on fellas. I fixed us a spot out behind the barn with some targets. Oh, grab that bucket of bullets and bring it, too."

Aaron picked the bucket up off the table, held it up, and laughingly said, "Hey, it's really called Bucket O' Bullets."

"Yeah, it's a good way to buy .22 ammo when you can find it. A few years ago, I'd see them all the time. Now, with all the craziness from this administration, there's been a buying frenzy on guns and ammo. But I always look whenever I'm out. Now, let's go do some plinking."

"Plinking?" Cameron said under his breath to his brother.

Aaron shook his head slightly. "No idea, but I think we're about to find out."

The boys had a ball. They found out that plinking is the term used for shooting at cans, bottles, old cookware, whatever the shooter's choice, and usually with a .22 caliber gun. Elliott had arranged all those things and more for the boys to shoot at. They liked the cookware and cans the best because they got to hear the metallic sound of the bullet hitting the piece. Aaron seemed to have a knack for it. He missed with his first shot and didn't miss again. Cameron struggled a bit at first.

Frustrated, he complained, "Dang it! I keep shooting high. What am I doing wrong?"

Aaron snickered. "Too many first-person shooter games would be my guess."

Elliott patted Cameron on the back and said, "You'll get it, Cam. Just remember what I told you about lining up the sights. You want the target sitting on top of your front sight. If you're shooting high, that means you're aiming high. Go ahead. Try it again."

Cameron took up the stance his grandfather had told him to use and aimed again. This time, he was rewarded with the sight of a soda can popping into the air and landing on the ground. "Finally!" he exclaimed. "Okay, zombies, I'm ready for you now!"

Aaron and Elliott laughed as Cameron strutted back and forth in front of them. "Okay, okay, zombie killer — I'd like to see you successfully hit a few more before you take on any moving targets. Try to hit a few more of them," Elliott said.

The reminder about the sights seemed to do the trick, as Cameron didn't miss again. Elliott smiled and said, "I think that'll do for now. You boys did real good. Let's head back up to the house and warm up a bit."

They checked on the livestock in the barn since they were already out there. Elliott found a few fresh eggs and placed them in his pocket. They threw some fresh hay in with the goats, then headed back to the house.

Once inside, Elliott checked the time. Seeing it was coming up toward noon, he decided to start on lunch. Washing his hands, he called out, "Guys, your first cooking lesson starts now. I'm gonna teach you how to make biscuits."

"The ones out of the can or the frozen ones? We know how to make those, Pap" Cameron said.

Elliott shook his head. "No, we're making biscuits from scratch. Pay attention now."

Elliott got out flour, goat's milk, and picked up a can off the back of the stove. Cameron and Aaron watched attentively. Using a sifter Elliott created a small pile of flour in his bowl.

"What is that thing, Pap?" Aaron asked.

"It's called a sifter," Elliott said. "It breaks up all the chunks in the flour and puts some air in it. Makes the biscuits fluffier."

Sticking a spoon inside the can, he scooped out a large spoonful of solid bacon grease and dropped it in a small cast-iron skillet sitting on the stove. He turned the burner on underneath it then went back to his bowl of flour. Using his hand, he created a small well in the center of the flour. He poured a bit of milk into the center and started working the flour into the milk with his hand.

"Now, you can use a spoon or a fork, but my granny and my mama always mixed their biscuits with their hand, so that's how I do it," Elliott said, as he continued forming a dough ball. He reached over and turned the heat off under the skillet. Using a well-worn potholder, he picked up the skillet and poured the melted bacon grease over his dough ball and continued mixing, working that in as well. "They both used buttermilk, and I wish I had some, but goat's milk is fine. You don't want to work the dough too much ... just enough to get everything mixed together. If you handle it too much, the biscuits will be tough."

He carried the bowl of dough over to the table. He pulled a large wood board from between the stove and the cabinet and laid it on the table. The boys could tell by looking at it that it was very old, and from the way he handled it, very dear to their grandfather. He took the sifter and sprinkled more flour over the board.

"You see that dip in the wood there in the middle?" Elliott asked, pointing to a slight depression in the center of the board. "This board belonged to my mama, and before that to her mama, my granny. There's been many a batch of biscuits, loaf of bread, pie crust, no telling what all worked on this board. So, you put some flour on it to keep the dough from sticking, plop your dough out on the board, sift some more flour over the top, then fold over a couple of times."

As he was talking, Elliott demonstrated the technique he used. Then, he took the edge of the dough and pulled a small section off. Rolling it between his hands he said, "They call this choking them off; I'm not real sure why. I guess it's because you kind of pull it from the rest with a choking motion." He demonstrated the move with an imaginary reach, then closed his hand into a fist. "Now, make a ball, pat it down a little to flatten it, then put it in your pan. Aaron, get that big skillet hanging on the wall and pour some of that bacon grease on the stove into it. Kind of tilt it around to cover the bottom."

Aaron did as he was told, then took the skillet to his grandfather. With floured hands, Elliott set the skillet next to the board on the table. He gently placed the first biscuit in the pan against the edge. Looking up at the boys, he asked, "Well, what are you waiting for? Give it a try. Get some flour on your hands first."

Cameron stepped in first, patted his hand in the flour on the board, then grabbed the edge of the dough. He pulled off a piece bigger than his fist and started rolling it. Elliott shook his head. "Nope, that's too big, Cam. Maybe a little more than half of that."

"But I like big biscuits, Pap," Cameron replied. "Yours is going to be about two bites, maybe three."

Elliott chuckled. "They puff up when they bake, just like the ones from the can. There you go, that's more like it."

Cameron had pulled about a third of the dough off and formed a ball with what was left. He patted it flat like he had seen his grandfather do then set it in the skillet about an inch away from the one Elliott had placed in it. Elliott picked Cameron's biscuit up and placed it next to his own. At the questioning look on his grandson's face, Elliott said, "They puff up better when they're right next to each other. I'm sure there's some kind of science behind that; all I know is it works. Your turn, Aaron."

Cameron stepped back with a satisfied grin on his face and watched his older brother perform the task. Aaron's attempt was almost identical to Elliott's, and Elliott congratulated him on doing it in one try. Aaron stood behind his grandfather and mouthed to Cameron, "Got it in one," holding up a flour-covered index finger as he did. Cameron held up a single finger at his brother, flipping him off, dropping it quickly when Elliott's head came up. In doing so, he rubbed his shirt and left a trail of flour down the front. Aaron snickered softly.

"Okay, you fellas finish them biscuits and I'll fry some country ham to go in them. Cameron, you've got flour on your shirt. That's a good sign. All good cooks are messy — at least that's what my mama always said." Elliott dusted his hands over the remaining dough. Cameron beamed at the comment.

The boys formed the remaining dough into biscuits and took the skillet to Elliott at the stove. Elliott placed it in the oven and walked the boys through how to clean up the area. The bowl he had made the dough in was lined in flour. He took it as is and placed it in the cabinet. He carried the dough board to the sink and brushed it off with his hand. He explained to the boys that the pieces worked best if only lightly cleaned.

Cameron asked, "How come you're showing us all this stuff now, Pap? We've been out here lots of times and you never showed us this stuff, or how you make biscuits, or how to shoot..."

Elliott looked lost in thought. Still, he replied, "I'm not sure why I never showed you how to do those things before. Maybe I thought your mom, or your grandma, would teach you how to cook. Boys need to know how to cook as much as girls do. As for the shooting, I knew how your mom felt about guns. I didn't want to step on anybody's toes. But everything is changed now. You need to know how to do all kinds of stuff you didn't before."

"You've got a lot of old stuff, Pap," Aaron remarked as he slid the board back into the spot where it was kept.

"Yep, I was an only child after my twin brother died when we was little, and so was my mama, so all their stuff came to me when they passed on. Your daddy was an only child, too, but I don't think he'd be interested in any of this stuff, so you boys can fight over it when I'm gone."

At the mention of their father, Cameron looked at Aaron. Aaron shook his head and mouthed the word "no" then turned his attention back to his grandfather. Cameron, however, had other ideas.

"Have you heard from him lately, Pap? Our dad?" Cameron asked, as his older brother stared daggers at him.

"As a matter fact, he called me a couple of weeks ago, out of the blue; hadn't heard from him in years," Elliott answered.

"Oh yeah? I wonder why," Cameron replied. Aaron was making a slashing motion at his throat. Cameron ignored him.

"Wondered that myself, so I flat out asked him. He said he missed his family, and he was calling to see if it would be all right if he stopped by sometime. I told him I reckoned that would be okay, then asked when he thought he might be coming. He said sometime soon but didn't say exactly when. I doubt he'll come; he said he was coming before and never did." There was a sadness in Elliott's tone as he spoke. Cameron started to speak, but Aaron cut him off.

"It's all right, Pap. We're here. Come on, Cam, let's get some more wood up on the back porch. We'll be back in a few minutes." Aaron nudged Cameron towards the back door. They put on their coats and walked out. Once they were away from the house, Aaron turned on his brother.

"I told you not to say anything," he said through gritted teeth. "What part of that did you not understand?"

Cameron was indignant. "You're not my boss! You can't tell me what to do! Didn't you see how sad Pap was talking about him? That's his son, his only child. Whether he was a shitty dad or not doesn't matter. Pap should know."

"Know what? That he's making promises to you, too, more broken promises? Cam, you'll just get his hopes up, then when Ethan doesn't show up — and he won't — it will be worse than if he never knew. Seriously, please don't say anything ... at least not now. We've got enough going on without bringing him into it." Aaron's voice had taken on a pleading tone.

Cameron sighed. "Fine, we'll do it your way, for now. But not forever. Just know that."

Aaron smiled at his little brother. "I can live with that. Let's go get that wood."

"You were serious about that? We hauled a shit ton in this morning."

"Apparently, this is our life now. Awesome, huh?"

Cameron shoved his hands deeper in his pockets as he started toward the shed. "Not in any way."

Chapter 16

Damon made good time until he got close to Baltimore. There were many more abandoned cars on the road which he was forced to weave around and even had to physically push a couple out of his path. The closer he got to the city limits, the more people he saw, and the more people who saw him. A functioning vehicle in an otherwise quiet area tends to attract attention. He decided it might be a good idea to try to skirt as much of the city as he could, so he got on the I-695 bypass. This would commit him to a long bridge crossing the Patapsco River, but being much further away from downtown, he hoped it would lead to fewer abandoned vehicles. There was an added benefit to the fact that he would pass a US Army Reserve Depot and a US Coast Guard facility before getting to the bridge. Hopefully, someone in one of those two places would know what kind of shape it was in before he committed to the crossing.

He stopped for a moment to look at a map of the area. While he could see the depot on the map, he couldn't see an easy way to get there as there wasn't an exit close. The Coast Guard area looked much more accessible, so he decided he would pull off there. He put the Humvee back in drive, instinctively checking for traffic, then continued down the highway.

That section of I-695, also known as the Baltimore Beltway, became a toll road soon after crossing Curtis Creek. Damon wondered for a moment whether he would have to break down the barrier that should be across the lane at the first tollbooth. When he reached it, he found that task had already been done by someone or something else. The arm was snapped off and lying beside the road.

Knowing there were other vehicles on the road, but not knowing who was in them, had him double checking the Sig and Beretta.

He took the exit for Quarantine Road then made a right on Hawkins Point Road. The first Coast Guard facility he came to was a logistics center. He figured that was as good a place as any to start.

Incoming traffic was barricaded to funnel past the guard shack, but the oncoming lane was still open, so Damon drove around. As he passed the guard shack on the other end, he saw that it was empty. He was not surprised to see a couple of vehicles in the parking lot in front of the logistics center. He parked, got out and locked the Humvee, and started for the door, the signed memo from General Everley in his hand. He had a feeling he would need it to get any information. Being met at the door by a Coast Guard police officer in full tactical gear told him he was right.

"Hold it right there. State your business, Major," the officer called out through the door.

Damon opened the folded paper and replied, "My mission is to get to New York City. I didn't want to go through Baltimore with everything that's happened. I was hoping someone here could let me know if the bridge is passable."

The officer peered through the door at the missive Damon held up for him to read. He gave a curt nod and said, "Very well, Sir," and unlocked the door. He held it open for Damon to enter and locked it behind them. Motioning down the hall, he said, "Captain Rogers is the first door on the left. I believe she has the information you're looking for." With that, the officer turned back and faced the door.

Damon knocked on the indicated door and was met with a terse, "Enter!" from the other side. He did and was met with a surprise. The volume of the voice had given him

131

a mental picture of a tall, mannish-built woman. She was anything but that. She stood when he came in and couldn't have been more than five feet tall. Dark blond hair was pulled back in a loose bun that seemed to be coming apart. She tugged at her shirt, which was a bit wrinkled, apparently trying to smooth it out. He was amazed at the big voice that had bellowed through the door from this little woman.

Captain Jeanna Rogers looked up as Damon came through the door. Seeing the gold oak leaves, she rose from her chair and stood at attention. Damon smiled and took the few steps across her small office with his hand outstretched.

"At ease, Captain," Damon said. "My name is Damon Sorley and I just need a quick minute of your time. I'm hoping to get some information from you regarding the state of the bridge across the river. I'm on my way to New York and getting stuck on a bridge that long is not on my itinerary."

Jeanna relaxed and shook his proffered hand. "Jeanna Rogers. My pleasure, Sir. Please have a seat," she replied, indicating the chair across from her.

Damon sat, taking in the simplistic decor and the tired-looking woman across from him. "Looks like you've had a long day already, Captain."

"Actually, a long night," she said. "I've been here since midnight. Doesn't look like my relief will be showing up anytime soon." She tried again to smooth the wrinkles from the front of her uniform shirt.

"Just you and CGPD out there manning this post?" Damon asked.

She nodded. "Sunday is usually the quietest night we have around here. I think we've taken quiet to a whole new level. Do you have any idea what the situation is, Sir?"

"I only know we were hit with an EMP in the upper atmosphere, that the whole country is in the dark, and that it was probably North Korea who did it."

She didn't try to hide the look of shock on her face. "Are you saying we're at war then?"

"So it would seem, but I don't know if there's been a declaration yet. Has anyone been by to brief you on your orders?"

She shook her head. "No one. We saw the flash about zero five hundred this morning then everything went dark. No cars, no choppers, nothing moving, even on the water. I sent Sloan down to the harbor and I hoofed it to the bridge. He said there were some folks wandering the docks but the few boats on the water seemed to be adrift. I put in a couple of miles on the bridge, but all the cars were sitting still." She paused then went on. "They always said it would never happen. That no one could get a missile close enough to do this to us. And yet here we are. This is going to be bad, isn't it, Sir?"

As much as Damon wanted to tell her how bad it truly could become, particularly in regard to the president and his agenda, he knew that wouldn't help anyone right now. Instead, he gave her a pat answer. "I don't know, Captain, but it certainly won't be good. Were you able to tell if the bridge is passable?"

"From what I could see, I think you can make it across. You might have to clear a couple of vehicles out of the way, but I'm sure that won't be a problem in the Humvee you're driving." At his raised eyebrow, she smiled and went on. "When the world is quiet, any sound gets your attention. I heard you pull up outside."

He nodded grimly and replied, "Yes, that's one of the reasons why I'd like to skirt around the big cities between here and New York. I don't want to get myself into a

133

situation where I'd have to fight to keep my ride, or worse, lose my ride in the fight."

"Well, this route will get you around Baltimore, but you've got Philadelphia after that. You have a plan for there as well?"

"I'll cross that bridge when I come to it, no pun intended," he said with a grin. He stood and extended his hand across the desk to her again. "Thank you for your time, Captain. Good luck to you. I think we're all going to need it."

She smiled at his first remark then her face turned solemn at the second as she shook his hand again. "I think you're right, Sir. God help us all."

He replied, "Let's hope so, but He's got his work cut out for Him."

As the captain had predicted, aside from some nudging to a few of the abandoned cars, Damon was able to cross the bridge. There were a few pedestrians crossing as well who tried to wave him down, but he didn't stop. Stopping would serve no purpose. He couldn't help them. He couldn't tell them much more than they should have figured out by themselves at that point, and he was on a mission.

He saw a country club to his left and wondered how long it would be until people could do leisurely things like that again. He was pretty sure no one would be taking the time to work on their putting for quite a while. To his right, the Back River seemed undisturbed by the upheaval the country had been thrust into. Mile after mile, everything he saw made him imagine what would become of that restaurant, that gas station, that sedan, that ski boat — things that no longer worked and, in the case of the vehicles, probably never would again. The electrical systems were toast, and even if the factories started back up tomorrow, it was likely it would cost more to replace the damaged parts than to just buy a new car. He couldn't fathom the effort it would take to clear all of them, nor where they would put them if they could. Billions of dollars in vehicles reduced to scrap metal in one blast. The thought was frustrating because it made him angry, yet he knew there was nothing he could do about it. He gripped the steering wheel a little tighter and continued on his way.

As the Beltway turned slightly in a northwesterly direction, he could see smoke to his right. The area was a mix of residential and commercial. The closer he got the thicker the smoke got. He slowed down to a crawl trying to see what was going on. Just before the tree line obscured his view, he could see what appeared to be multiple mobile homes on fire. He had just passed the ramp that went that direction, and it had a lot of people on it who seemed to be trying to get away from the fires. Seeing his military vehicle, they rushed toward him waving their hands, screaming for him to stop. He didn't. In fact, he sped up, narrowly missing a couple of teenagers who had almost made it to the Humvee. He stared straight ahead but glanced into the rearview mirror to see them chasing him and flipping him off. One picked a beer bottle up from the side of the road and threw it at him. It didn't come close to hitting him, but he didn't slow down again except to get around dead vehicles.

When he got near the interchange that would put him back on I-95, he passed a parking lot that served a Home Depot, Walmart, and Sam's Club. There were people everywhere carrying off items that had obviously been looted from the stores. Even with the windows up, he could hear them yelling at each other, fighting over supplies in panic-laced voices. When they heard the engine of the Humvee, many heads turned in his direction. He heard a gunshot, then another, then screaming from the crowd. He pressed the gas pedal harder and drove as fast as the stalled cars would allow to get away from the chaos that he knew had just begun.

This is the outskirts of Baltimore, nowhere near downtown. What is Philly going to be like? Even worse, what about New York? The thoughts going through his mind were not comforting. He decided he would pull off at the next spot he found with no one around to take another look at the map. *I need to find a way around Philly first. If I make it out of there, then I'll worry about New York. Big if.*

Chapter 17

Will figured they had about two miles to get to the Kroger at Appling and Summer Avenue. He thought briefly about trying to figure a way to skirt around the area since he was sure it would be as bad, if not worse, than Walmart, but the Bartlett Police department was right next door, so he hoped they would have that place under control if nothing else.

They kept up a slow but steady pace through the industrial/commercial area. Will wasn't surprised that they didn't run into anyone on the way. There wasn't really anything on that road that should interest looters. They also kept up a steady conversation, each sharing with the other stories about their families, friends, and lives. Will was entranced with this woman, and he felt — actually, hoped — the feeling was mutual. The two miles passed quickly.

There was no mistaking when they got close to the large grocery store. The number of people in the area was much greater than the quiet commercial street they had just been on. Apparently, folks had figured out this was something more than ice on the power lines. The ones he had encountered on the highway hadn't put all the pieces together yet, not that soon. As more and more people added up the things that weren't working, they had no choice but to come to the conclusion that this wasn't going to end today, tomorrow, or even next week. With those ideas came the realization that most of them were woefully unprepared for a situation such as they now found themselves in. Their survival instinct went into overdrive, and they headed to the closest store to try to get food for themselves and their families ... along with hundreds of others in the area.

Will had never seen anything like it. People were pushing and shoving each other to get closer to the door, and the closer they got to the entrance of the store, the more concentrated the number of bodies were that were trying to get in. At the entrance, which was closed and apparently locked, the mob was so thick no one could move. They were yelling at someone inside the store.

"We see you in there! Open these doors! We have a right to that food in there! You can't keep it all to yourself!" This was immediately followed by the sound of fists and unknown objects hitting the glass doors. Will had a feeling he knew where this was going to go and was about to steer Amanda away from the store when they heard a gunshot. That sound, along with the sound of shattering glass, left no doubt some of them had taken matters into their own hands to gain access to the supplies inside. Then they heard screaming and saw people running away from the store. Unable to avert their gaze, Will and Amanda watched as the crowd thinned out, leaving just a couple of men standing at the broken door staring inside, the rest of the people having retreated to what they seemed to consider a safe distance. One held a pistol, the other a shotgun. The man with the pistol was speaking.

"Now, that was an accident. I wasn't trying to hurt anybody. That little gal ran right into my line of fire. I'm real sorry, but we need that food to feed our families. So, y'all just need to step back, let us get what we came for, and call it a day."

A voice from inside the store yelled back, "What about Lauren's family? They needed their daughter! Is some food more important than her life? What is wrong with you people?"

The man with the shotgun replied calmly, "In case you hadn't noticed, everything's gone to shit. Ain't nothing gonna be more important than food and water — well, except maybe guns and ammo. So, you gotta hang on to all the food and water you find. Now, do like the man said and step back unless you want someone else to get hurt."

The people inside must've done as they were told, because the two men holding the guns walked in followed by a throng, still keeping their distance yet driven to acquire the supplies they came for. Will and Amanda watched the bizarre scene from the edge of the parking lot. Will turned to Amanda, who seemed to be in shock.

"Are you okay?" he asked.

Amanda slowly shook her head. "No, I most decidedly am not okay. They shot someone! Where are the police? Their station is right next door, for God's sake!"

"I don't think the police are going to be doing a lot of law enforcing for a while," Will replied. "They likely have families to feed, too. Priorities are changing every second. Come on, let's get going and get away from here. We only have a couple more —"

Will was cut off when a voice behind them spoke. "We'll be taking those packs and any cash you have on you."

They turned to see two men, one with a pistol and one with a revolver, both pointed at them. Amanda's hand flew up to her mouth to stifle a scream. "Hand them over nice and slow and nobody gets hurt."

Will tried to think fast for a way out of the situation, but he found it was hard to concentrate with a gun pointed at him. He figured it couldn't hurt to at least try to reason with them.

"Look, fellas, I've got some cash I'll give you, but we really need the packs. It's just a few bottles of water, some protein bars, and spare clothing. We've been walking for miles, and we still have a few to get home. Here, I'll show you." With that, he took his pack off, unzipped the main compartment, and pulled it open so they could see inside. "See? It's just some stuff I had with me in the car when I got stranded on the highway. I do have a couple of hundred bucks though." He pulled his wallet out of his back pocket, opened it up, and pulled out the bills he had put in it just a few hours before. He held them out to the men, and the one with the revolver snatched the money from his hand. With his wallet in his left hand, he stuck his right into the front pocket of his jeans and pulled out another stack. He held that out to the men, and the one holding the pistol took those.

Looking at each other like they held winning lottery tickets, the two men looked back at them and pistol man replied, "Is that all you got? You ain't holding out on us, are you?"

Trying to look nonchalant, Will shrugged his shoulders. "That's it, man. I try to carry two hundred bucks cash when I'm on the road. You've got it all."

This seemed to appease the men, as they lowered their weapons while stuffing the bills in their pockets. Revolver man said, "All right, you can keep the packs. No hard feelings, but it's every man for himself now, you know?"

Will nodded and said, "I understand. Thanks, guys. We're heading out now. Good luck to you." With that, he took Amanda by the arm and steered her away from the men. She hadn't said a word through the entire ordeal. She remained silent as they crossed Summer Avenue and finally found her voice in front of a bank about a half a block away from the confrontation. She stopped dead in her tracks and looked Will in the eye.

"You thanked them. They robbed you and you thanked them. Why would you do that?"

Will sighed and said, "Because they didn't take our packs. Because they believed me when I told them that was all the cash I had. It wasn't, by the way. And because they didn't shoot us. Believe me, that was not my first instinct. But I'm smart enough to know that I can't take on two guys with guns barehanded. You've heard the term pick your battles? That wasn't one we could win."

Amanda seemed to consider what he had said. "I guess I see what you're saying. Just between you and me, this situation is getting worse by the minute. I'm glad I wasn't by myself. I don't know what I would've done if you hadn't been there, Will. I'm so glad you were."

Will looked at her solemnly. "I'm glad I was, too, but it definitely tells me we need to pay very close attention to our surroundings, especially since we're getting back into a residential area. We're less than a mile from my parents' place but it's all houses between here and there. Just keep your eyes open and let me know if you see anything … I don't know, weird … out of place. I'm sure we'll know it if we see it."

"Do you really think we'll run into something else, or someone else like those guys back there?" she asked, voice full of concern.

"I'd bet the rest of the cash I have stashed on it. Hang on a sec."

Will set his backpack on the frozen sidewalk and opened one of the side pockets. He pulled out the multi-tool and opened it to the small knife blade. Zipping his pack up and slinging it over his shoulder, he picked up the implement and said, "I know it wouldn't have helped against those guns, but there's no telling what we may still come across before we get there. Looks like a decent crowd up ahead at the Dollar Tree. Let's try to get through there quick. Keep your eyes forward and walk like you've got someplace to be." He placed the tool gently in his coat pocket.

"We do have someplace to be," Amanda replied.

Will nodded. "And I'd like to get there in one piece, today."

Chapter 18

As the afternoon progressed, the snow fall ceased, leaving them in a winter wonderland that was bitterly cold. The fireplace produced enough heat to push the chill out of the living room, so Carly and her parents were pretty much camping out there. Lauri had brought the camp stove in and placed it on the hearth. Joel was sitting in his recliner with a pen and paper working on something. Carly seemed to be lost in thought.

"What are you writing, Joel?" Lauri asked.

Joel looked up from his paper after he finished what he had been in the process of writing. "Lists of stuff we need to do and plan for. I'm also trying to figure out some way to get us all to Elliott's place after Will gets home. We could do it in the riding mower with the trailer — it would take the weight — but it's not a really secure way to travel, and we couldn't take much else with us. At this point, I just don't know how we can get twenty miles from here without some kind of transportation. Your knees could never make a trip like that walking. I thought I was going to pass out after going just two miles to Carly's. We aren't in any shape for that kind of activity."

"No, we aren't, but if that's the only option, what other choice do we have?" Lauri replied.

"I'm still working on it. We've got a little time."

"Speaking of time, do you think we should hook up the generator and let the fridge and freezer run for a little while?"

Joel's eyebrows raised. "Crap, I hadn't even thought of that. Yes, we should. I just hate that everybody is going to know about it then. It's one thing to lend out an old chainsaw. It's a whole other one to have someone want to borrow your generator."

"Just say no, Dad," Carly commented from the couch sharply. Both of her parents looked at her in surprise at her tone. "You've spent the whole day so far helping other people, including me. Especially me. Of course, I'm your daughter. They're just your neighbors. You've helped them do stuff they should already know how to do. You've tried to educate them on what they should be doing. They're not your responsibility. Your family comes first, and that food in there will feed your family. I say fire it up, and we'll turn them away as they come to the door."

Lauri looked at Carly in shock. "Carly, what in the world has gotten into you? You were snarky when Jack was here, and it seems you're getting worse."

Carly shrugged. "What's the point, Mom? Everything is shit now. Our whole world has been vaporized. Do you know what was going to happen to me next year? I was going to be made a partner in our firm. A partner! My life was about to take a turn for the awesome. Now? It's all gone. My savings, my job, my car, my life — with the push of a button. No more grocery stores, no more cute boots, or mani/pedi spa days. No more pizza or hamburgers. No more fun!" She paused in her rant, then went on. "And on top of everything else, my boys are a thirty-minute drive away that I can't make. Plus, Will should have been here hours ago. Where is he?"

Joel interjected, "Carly, you just need to settle down now. We have things we need to do —"

"I've tried to settle down, Dad! I can't! The enormity of this situation is just too much! It's all gone! Everything we knew, everything we had — just gone! How is that possible? And why didn't anybody plan for something like this? Why did the government leave us vulnerable to an attack like what we have apparently experienced? Isn't that

143

part of their job, to protect us, and this country, from attacks?"

Carly was on a rampage, and her parents just sat and stared. They seemed to be waiting for her to get it out of her system. When she didn't go on, Joel replied quietly, "Honey, I understand where you're coming from. It is a bit overwhelming to think about what life is going to be like. Honestly, we probably have no idea how bad it's going to get. All we can do is get through it. Together. We've all lost everything just like you have. But melting down is not the answer. It won't fix this. It won't help. We need to work on what we can do right now, what we can do in the next hour, and then the one after that. When Will gets here, then we'll figure out the next step."

He watched as her face changed from anger to anguish. The tears started to fall, slowly at first, then harder. She was crying so hard that her breath was coming in great gasps. Both he and Lauri went to their daughter, sitting on either side of her on the sofa. They both put their arms around her as she let out the despair that had been building inside her, probably since Joel first showed up at her door that morning. They knew how she felt about Aaron and Cameron, the not knowing what they were dealing with or how they were faring, since their own son was still not home. Half of their family was not with them and they had no idea how they were doing, or if they were okay. They were pretty sure the boys were fine with Elliott, but Will was a big unknown. Lauri patted her back as Carly's tears continued to flow.

"There you go, baby, let it out. It's going to be all right. The most important thing is we're together. Will is on his way home. I bet he'll be walking through that door any minute. And we will get to the boys. Don't you doubt that for one second."

Carly hiccupped as she looked at her mother. "How? On a riding lawn mower, pulling a trailer?"

Joel replied resolutely, "If that's what it takes."

Once Carly had cried out her frustrations, she went to the bathroom to wash her face while Joel pulled the generator out and hooked it up to the house. He had Lauri turn off all the breakers inside except the refrigerator and freezer. He pulled the cord a couple of times and the old generator coughed, then caught. It was loud, and Joel grimaced at the noise. He had forgotten how loud it was. *Oh well,* he thought, *nothing to be done about it now.* He went back inside and checked that everything was working as it should. He heard the compressor on both appliances humming.

Joel stood in the kitchen listening to appliances. "Well, that looks good and sounds even better. You don't realize how much ambient noise there is until it's gone. We'll let it run for at least an hour. Lauri, honey, if there's anything you want to pull out for supper, now would be the time to do that. We should probably follow my advice to Jack and work on the fridge first. The freezer is pretty full, isn't it?"

Lauri nodded. "Yes, it is. I think it will be okay for a few days as long as we get some power to it from time to time. There's a chuck roast in the fridge I was going to cook for Sunday dinner but with no range ..."

"Thick or thin? The roast I mean," Joel said.

"Pretty thin. It would have cooked in just a couple of hours in a cast iron Dutch oven."

Joel smiled. "Go ahead and get it ready. I'll get you someplace to cook it." With that, he donned his coat and went out to the backyard.

Lauri got the roast out and put it in the Dutch oven with carrots, potatoes, and onions. She had just finished adding her secret ingredient — onion soup mix — and water when

Joel came back inside. She placed the lid on the pot and wiped her hands on a dish towel. Joel picked up the heavy cooking implement and headed back to the door. Lauri hurried around him to open it for him. She stopped and asked, "Where are you going with it, honey? How are you going to cook it?"

Grinning, he replied, "Open the door and you'll see."

She opened the door to find the gas grill pulled up close to the house. Joel set the pot down and opened the lid. He placed the Dutch oven on the rack and closed the back over it. He adjusted the flames down to a medium setting then went back inside. Lauri asked, "Will it be alright to cook in there? I've never cooked with cast iron in a grill before."

"Of course it will. You cooked in cast iron over a fire when we used to go camping. Same thing, except we can regulate it better in the grill because we can turn it up or down and we have a thermometer in the lid so it's more like the oven."

"That's brilliant, dear! I wonder if I can make bread in there." Lauri looked thoughtful at her comment.

"I don't know if we're going to be able to stay here long enough to find out. I'm afraid —" A knock at the door interrupted him.

Joel opened the door to find Beth standing there again. This time she had on warmer clothes. Joel said, "Beth, if your fire is out I'm sorry, but I don't have any more wood to spare. Maybe you could gather dropped limbs or something in your yard."

Beth was looking toward the sound coming from the generator. She looked back at Joel. "What? Oh, no, it's still burning. Actually, I was wondering if I could borrow your generator. I heard it running from inside my house. If I could run the furnace for a bit and warm the whole house up, it would be much more comfortable. I could also cook some dinner. It would probably only take a couple of hours.

I could let you know when I'm done, and you could come get it."

Joel stared at her then shook his head. "No, Beth, you can't borrow my generator. As you can hear, we're using it. Besides, it isn't powerful enough to run your furnace or your stove. Those are two hundred twenty-volt appliances. That generator is only good for one hundred ten-volt stuff. Either way, it isn't something I would lend to anybody, not now."

"Well, I just thought you would want to help your neighbors out," Beth commented indignantly. "You know, come together, pool our resources, especially since you seem to think this is going to last for a while. Doesn't it make sense to get with everyone close and make sure we are all fed and warm?"

"Maybe. Tell me, Beth, what will you be bringing to the group?" Joel asked.

"Well ... I ... um ... I'm a great organizer. I can find out what everyone has that can be used by the group. I can see who has what skills to offer. Like you, Joel. You obviously know about fire starting."

Joel squinted at her. "And what do you have that could be used by the group? Any large amounts of canned goods, maybe food in your freezer? Trees we can cut down for firewood?"

Beth shook her head. "No, not really. I have a few things, but it's probably only enough for me for a couple of days. I needed to go to the store and was actually planning to go tomorrow after the roads cleared a bit. I did try to start my car and it's dead. So, I'm going to be needing some help to get through this. You all have all the food Lauri cans, and chickens out back, and you know how to do things, Joel ..." Her voice tapered off.

"We don't know yet how long this is going to last, Beth. If we eat everything we have now, we'll all be starving in a month."

Beth looked shocked. "A month? Why in God's name do you think this will take a month to fix? Surely, we aren't talking longer than a week, two at the most."

Joel shook his head. "I don't think so. You have a gas grill, right? You could cook on that like you would a gas stove. Just fire it up and set the pans right on the grate."

"Do you have any idea how much I paid for my cookware, Joel?" Beth asked with a look of distaste. "It's not for using over an outdoor grill. Perhaps you all have an older pot or pan I could borrow, at least for cooking with."

"So, basically, you're asking us to take care of you," Carly said coming around the corner. "No, I get it. If it weren't for my parents here I'd be in the same boat as you. Hell, I'd *be* you."

"Carly …" Joel said softly.

"No, no, it's okay, Dad. I get where she's coming from. But the problem, Beth, is that this isn't just going to last for a week or so," Carly went on. "According to my dad, it's going to last for *years*. Years! Can you even fathom that? I've known all day and I still can't believe it. So, unless you are willing to get your hands dirty — literally — and learn how to grow food, you're going to die. Plain and simple. Oh, and that's *if* you can get your hands on some seeds, and *if* you have any idea how to garden, and *if* you have the equipment to preserve it, which let's face it, we all know you don't. You won't even use your fancy cookware to feed yourself. That brings us back to you're probably going to die unless you can find someone to take care of you. Well, sorry to tell you, sister, but that isn't going to be us."

Lauri cried out, "Carly!"

Carly turned to her mother. "What, Mom? Shall we sugar coat it instead and send her home with some of your

148

canned green beans and tell her everything will be fine in a few days? Because that's a lie. You taught me not to lie. Unless she's willing to work, she's gonna die. Period." With that, Carly left and headed for the kitchen.

Lauri's face was beet red as she looked at Beth. "Beth, I'm sorry about Carly's behavior. Her sons are at their other grandfather's house up in Tipton County, and she's distraught over not knowing if they're okay, or how to get to them."

Beth looked down her nose at both of them. "She was very rude. There's no excuse for bad manners like that —"

"Now you hold on right there, Beth," Joel interrupted her. "Lauri just told you why she's acting that way and that *is* a good excuse, especially on a day like today. If you had kids you'd understand. And FYI, everything she said is true. So, I'd suggest you march yourself back home and try to figure out how not to starve to death. Good luck with that." He had never invited her in, so she still stood out on the porch. He started to close the door, but she reached up and placed a hand on it.

In a slightly whiny voice, she said quietly, "I don't know what to do. I don't know where to start."

Joel looked her in the eye. "Get those fancy pans of yours and cook everything in your fridge that's going to spoil out on your gas grill. That's a good place to start. Make what you've got last as long as you can. Good luck. You're gonna need it." Joel shut the door without giving her a chance to respond. Lauri was still red-faced. Joel put a hand on her arm. "Carly's right. No need to lie or beat around the bush. Most of these people are probably going to die in the next month or so."

"Are you saying we should just stand by and watch that happen, Joel?"

He shook his head. "No, we won't watch it because we won't be here. As soon as Will gets home, we're leaving."

"How?" she asked, shock apparent in her voice.
"I'll let you know as soon as I figure that out."

Chapter 19

Elliott lived on Tracy Road, close to the end, by Highway 14. When he had built his house forty odd years before, there were very few people out there. With the growth of Memphis and its suburbs, folks had fled to the adjoining counties to buy homes. While there weren't neighbors right on top of him, they were a lot closer now than they were back then. Many times through the years he had considered selling the place to move further into the country, but he could never quite bring himself to do it. He and his wife, Judy, had designed and built that house, and even though she had died of cancer when Ethan was ten, he felt he would be betraying her memory to let it go. Plus, he often thought he could feel her presence in the house.

The house was built ranch-style; that is, all one level. They called it a cabin, because it had a log exterior rather than siding. The interior looked pretty much the same as it had for the past forty years. Judy had chosen the paint, flooring, and cabinets; almost everything inside had her hand on it. A few more reasons why he couldn't let it go.

In lieu of fencing, Elliott had planted pine trees along the property line for a sense of privacy when other houses started going up nearby. His driveway came straight from the road then curved to the right to go into the carport. Another row of pines shielded the house and yard from the road. Those trees had been in the ground for thirty years. There was no gate, but anyone trying to see the place would have to come up a gravel driveway, and they were not going to be able to do that quietly. Not in a car or truck anyway.

With the tree lines in place, Elliott couldn't see his neighbors and they couldn't see him. But when they were outside shooting, Elliott and the boys could be heard. Not that Elliott cared — he was shooting his guns on his property in the direction of the state land that joined his on that side. There was no one for miles that way.

Elliott had come out on the porch to check on the boys' progress with the wood when he heard the sound of rocks crunching under wheels coming up the driveway. Aaron and Cameron were on their way back from the shed. Aaron was pushing a wheelbarrow loaded down with cut wood. Cameron had the wood tote bag from the house full, bringing up the rear. Elliott slipped into his coat, walked down the steps of the back porch, and headed out to the driveway to see what the sound was. He was surprised to see his neighbor, Roger Harrison, struggling to ride a bike up the gravel drive.

Roger came to a slippery stop in front of Elliott. Gasping for air, he said, "Hey ... Elliott ... give ... me ... just ... a ... sec ... to ... catch ... my ... breath ..." He stopped, overcome with a coughing spell.

Elliott chuckled and slapped him on the back. "Aren't you a little old to be bike riding, much less in the snow, Roger?"

Still trying desperately to take a deep breath, the fifty-something-year-old man nodded. After a moment, with a huge sigh, Roger was able to speak. "Hell, yeah, I'm too old, and too out of shape, but it was the only thing with wheels at my house that would run. I figured if anybody would know what was going on it'd be you, so I told Cindy I was gonna ride over here after I heard you shooting this morning. That was a half hour ago."

"Good Lord, Roger, you could've walked faster than that. Where'd you get the bike anyway?"

"It was supposed to be my grandson's Christmas present. My son, Jeff, left it at our house to keep it hid until

Christmas. Just so you know, you might still be able to ride a bike, but you're probably not good at it anymore."

Elliott laughed out loud at that. "Give yourself a break, Roger. Riding a bike in the snow wouldn't be easy for anybody. How about a cup of coffee?"

"That would be awesome," Roger replied. "Let me just park this contraption up by the porch."

Aaron and Cameron had reached them by then. Elliott turned to them and said, "Boys, this is my neighbor, Roger Harrison. Roger, these are my grandsons, Aaron and Cameron Marshall."

Aaron set the wheelbarrow down as Cameron walked up and set the bag on the back porch. They both shook Roger's hand. "Very pleased to meet you, sir," Aaron said. Cameron commented the same.

"Pleased to meet you fellas, too. Now, how about that coffee, Elliott? I'm about froze to death," Roger said, shivering as if to prove his point.

"Come on inside. I've got some warming on the wood stove. Aaron, you can dump that wheelbarrow right there. Cam, go ahead and bring that tote inside."

"Yes, sir," the boys replied in unison. With that, they all went in, stamping their feet to dislodge the snow from their boots on the porch. Inside, coffee was poured for the adults, while the boys had instant hot chocolate. Settling down in the warm living room with their hot drinks, Roger posed the question he had ridden over to ask.

"So, do you? Know what's happened, that is?"

Elliott shook his head. "Not for positive, but I've got an idea."

Roger waited. When Elliott didn't expound on his statement, Roger said, "Well? Are you going to tell me, or you just going to leave me hanging here?"

Elliott remained quiet while thoughts raced through his head. Roger, and his wife, Cindy, had lived next to Elliott

153

for twenty years. They invited Elliott over for cookouts three or four times a year. They were friends, possibly could be considered good friends, but not exactly close friends. They knew Elliott grew and canned his own vegetables because he shared his canned goods with them. They knew he hunted because he brought them venison every year. They didn't know he planned for possible disaster situations.

While he wasn't an extremist, Elliott could have been considered a bit of a prepper. He usually kept at least six months' worth of canned goods, store-bought or home-canned, and usually a combination of the two, along with a large chest freezer that was mostly full of meat, along with some vegetables that froze better than they canned. He had made sure he could get water from his well, even without electricity, and he never let his propane tank get less than half full. He had enough seasoned wood in the shed to last into next winter, even if they had to use the wood stove to cook. He had livestock that provided food and could be food if needed.

"Well, to be perfectly honest with you, Roger, I think somebody hit us with an EMP," Elliott finally said matter-of-factly.

Roger sat looking at him blankly. Finally, he replied, "Huh?"

Elliott spent the next ten or fifteen minutes relaying to Roger what he knew about EMPs. Roger didn't ask any questions until he sensed Elliott was done.

"Ho-lee shit," Roger finally said. "You're serious, aren't you? You really think we've been attacked?"

Elliott shrugged. "It would explain all that has happened this morning. You tell me — what else takes out the power, cars, phones, everything?"

"Wait, how do you know about this stuff? Why do you know about it?" Roger asked, incredulously.

"Because I don't trust our government to tell us everything we should and need to know. Because anything can happen at any time. Earthquakes, tornadoes, floods, just to name a few. Because I talked to people who were in New Orleans during Katrina and heard what the police and city government did and didn't do. I wanted to be able to take care of myself if there was an emergency or a disaster. I didn't plan well for this one though. Didn't really think it was possible for someone to kill everything electronic. Yet, here we are."

At this point, Roger was looking scared. "What ... I mean, I don't know ... what do you think we should do now?"

Elliott stood, went over to the wood stove, picked up the coffee pot, and walked back over to Roger. He poured fresh coffee in his friend's cup, and replied, "Live. Just do the best we can. There's not much else to do."

"Live how? No electricity for God knows how long. No food at the grocery store because there's no more deliveries, but that doesn't matter because no more gas for the cars and the cars don't run anyway. I'm sure we can figure out how to live without electricity, but nobody lives without food and water. We aren't set up like you, Elliott. No power means no water at our house since we have a well, too. We probably have one to two weeks' worth of food. Then what? I don't know how to hunt. Hell, I don't even have a rifle or a shotgun. What are we going to do?"

Elliott was still standing beside him and laid a hand on his friend's shoulder. "I can help with some of that, Roger. You can get water from my well. I'll even give you one of these containers I have to haul it in. Maybe you can figure out a way to strap it on that bike you rode over here. Hell, I found out my old tractor runs so we can use that as long as we have fuel. If you want to learn, I can teach you how to hunt. In the spring, I can share some seeds with you, so you can plant a garden. You and Cindy will have to learn how to cook over an open fire. If you don't have any cast-iron cookware, it will be harder for you, but you can still do it. Yeah, we can live without electricity. Plenty of folks before us did. But they were set up for it with cook stoves, lanterns, that kind of thing. Most people don't have things like that anymore. All we can do is try."

Roger gazed into his coffee cup as if it could somehow magically fix the issue. After a moment, he looked up at Elliott and said softly, "I'd really appreciate any help you can give us, Elliott. Otherwise, we'll be dead in a month."

Elliott patted Roger on his shoulder. "That's not gonna happen. We'll figure it out. Now, let's go take a look at that bike and see how we can rig it to carry 40 pounds of water."

In the end, they couldn't come up with a way to attach anything to the bike that could hold the heavy water jug. Roger told Elliott they had a good bit of bottled water and would probably be all right for a day or so. He said he'd look around at his place to see if he could figure something out, and Elliott promised to do the same. Roger said he needed to get home to Cindy to tell her what Elliott had shared and start figuring out what they needed to do now. Elliott told him he would check back in with them in a couple of days. The three of them watched as he struggled to ride the bike through the snow and ice down the drive.

Aaron looked at his grandfather and said, "Do you think they'll make it, Pap?"

Elliott looked thoughtful then replied, "They will, because we're going to help them."

"Do you think we'll make it, Pap?" Cameron asked, voice full of concern. "I mean, all of us? Mom, Nana, Pops, and Uncle Will?"

Elliott laid a hand on the arm of each of his grandsons. "I have no doubt we will all be fine. They'll get here, I know they will. If they don't, we'll go get them. And you know what? We need to start getting ready for that. Let's go inside and make room for four more people in our family."

Chapter 20

Right before reaching Wilmington, Damon chose the 295 bypass which would take him into New Jersey after crossing the Delaware River. From there, he took the New Jersey Turnpike which passed through both rural and suburban areas. Though it was another toll road, none of the barriers were intact. He was still able to maneuver relatively easily around the dead vehicles littering the highway. He was pretty sure that would change when he got to a major city.

The closer he got to the outskirts of Philadelphia, the more urban the surrounding area became. He had topped off the fuel tank when he stopped to check his map and was fairly certain he had enough diesel to get him all the way to New York. At least, that was his hope. He certainly didn't want to have to stop and try to find fuel anywhere between Philly and New York. The area was heavily populated, and he knew he didn't stand a chance if a large group tried to commandeer his vehicle.

Just past Parkville Station Road, he came into a densely populated area. Even though it was bitterly cold out, there were people milling about in the neighborhoods he could see on either side of the highway. As before, the sound of the Humvee's engine garnered more attention than he wanted but the tree line on either side of the road provided a bit of a barrier between him and the people who were outside. He kept his speed steady and didn't slow down for anything or anyone.

The upside to this area of the Turnpike was that there weren't a lot of exits. Consequently, he didn't have to constantly watch on and off ramps for danger. The downside was that it made a perfect chokepoint for an ambush. If you saw one up ahead there was really no way to avoid it unless you were willing to drive into the thick tree line on either side of the road. Damon didn't know if things like that were going on yet, but he had to consider worst-case scenarios; and that was one of them.

The light snow that had been falling when he left DC was getting heavier the further north he went. Tire tracks in the road in front of him were being covered over with the falling snow. Whoever had busted through the barricades at the toll booths had done so hours before. The fact that they had a running vehicle told him they were either military or a civilian with a car or truck that was at least forty years old.

He had come across people walking on the highway who tried to flag him down. Every time he would move to the other side of the road, not slowing any or acknowledging their presence. He could see them railing at him in the rearview mirror. He wished he could help but he knew he couldn't. And he had a mission. One that, if successful, could save his beloved country. If he failed, they would be left with a shadow of their nation.

He had let his mind wander contemplating the repercussions of his success or failure, so it took a moment to register that there was something blocking the highway ahead. He instinctively let his foot off the gas as he peered through the falling snow trying to see what the obstruction was. Checking that there was no one around to assault him, he came to a stop. He was less than half a mile from exit three. Beneath the overpass, there were cars blocking all the lanes in both directions. It was too much of a coincidence that people would have filled all four lanes directly under the overpass when the pulse hit. Someone had done this deliberately.

Damon let the Humvee inch forward slowly as he tried to make out where the people were who had to be there.

Just before the exit ramp he saw a head pop up, then another. Movement on the overpass got his attention. Two more men appeared with some kind of semi-automatic rifles pointed in his direction. Not good. Not good at all. He pulled the Beretta from under the seat and set it beside him, then took the Sig out of its holster and placed it in his lap.

Damon quickly weighed his options. Stopping wasn't one of them. Though he wasn't familiar with the area, he knew he'd have a better chance on the ramp. Ramming the vehicles blocking the road was an option, but there was also a possibility it could disable the Humvee. Slight, but still possible. His decision made, Damon pushed the gas pedal to the floor and headed for the ramp.

This action apparently caught the pirates under the ramp off guard. They scrambled from behind the vehicles they had been using for cover. Their counterparts on the overpass were in a better position and started firing on the Humvee. Bullets hitting the metal body only made Damon instinctively duck as he made the curve that would take him directly to them. Just as the ramp started to rise to make it pass over the Turnpike, Damon blasted through the guard rail, yelling, "Shit!" while cutting a path through the deep snow between the road and the tree line. The large tires sent up a plume of white behind him as he slid to the right, very nearly hitting a tree, then to the left taking out a sign on the side of the road. As he headed away from what could have been a deadly confrontation, he was thankful for the armored body and bullet-resistant glass of the vehicle he was in. He heard the bullets pinging in the back until he got outside their range.

Even though his hands were shaking uncontrollably, he didn't stop or even slow down until he got to a commercial area about a mile further down the road. Looking in all directions and seeing no one, he let the Humvee coast to a stop.

Damon closed his eyes and took several deep breaths in an attempt to slow his heart rate out of the cardiac arrest range. He pulled a water bottle out of the pack on the seat beside him and took a good long drink. He knew something like this could happen; expected it, in fact. However, in the thick of it, his mind took him back to his days in Afghanistan when a short drive from point A to point B could be the last trip you made. Unseen danger was everywhere. Situations like he had just gotten himself out of were common occurrences there. You never approached an abandoned vehicle or an unknown national without extreme caution. Even that was sometimes not enough. While he was there, he often thought to himself, *man, I'm glad I don't have to live like this. I feel sorry for these people in these conditions.* Now he and everyone else in the country would get a taste of what that life was like.

He gave himself a few more minutes as he looked at the map again. The Turnpike was angling away from Philadelphia. He hoped that meant it would take him through less populated areas. Fewer people equaled fewer problems in his mind. He started back down the road, eyes constantly scanning in all directions for problems. His thoughts were further away though. *If I ran into something like that outside of Philly, what will it be like in downtown New York City?*

~~~~~

Olstein had issued everyone at the meeting that morning a satellite phone, or sat phone as they were called, on the premise that they needed to communicate with each other. In reality, it was so that he could keep tabs on all of them. After repeated attempts to contact Admiral Stephens with no success, he next called General Everley. Everley answered on the second ring.

"Everley," he said into the phone.

"This is President Olstein. I'm looking for an update on our troop recall from all branches of our military. I need a status report," he said in response.

Charles rolled his eyes and replied, "Sir, this is not a five-minute thing. It will take weeks, possibly months, to bring all of our assets back to this country. Orders have to be issued, arrangements have to be made; there are a lot of moving parts in this scenario. Plus, we're at a disadvantage in our bases here at home because communications have been severely damaged. Orders will have to be hand-delivered in some cases. This is going to take a while."

"We need this to happen as quickly as possible, General," Olstein remarked rudely. "By the way, have you talked to Admiral Stephens since the meeting this morning? I've tried calling him multiple times and there's no answer. The Navy should be easier to round up since a lot of them were not in the blast zone."

Everley pressed his lips together firmly then lied and said, "No, I haven't seen him. If I do, I'll tell him you're looking for him."

"If you see him, you tell him to call me immediately. We're in the middle of the worst crisis this country has ever faced, and I can't find one of my joint Chiefs. That is unacceptable!" he barked into the phone.

Knowing Arthur was probably well on his way to Tennessee by now, Charles smiled to himself. "I'll do that, Mr. President. Is there anything else?"

"I want regular updates on the troops return. I shouldn't have to call and ask for them."

"As soon as I have something to report, I'll report it …
Sir." Charles couldn't hide the contempt in his voice but apparently the president hadn't picked up on it.

"See that you do, General!" Olstein abruptly ended the call.

Charles tossed the phone onto his desk. "Putz." He picked the phone back up and put a call into Damon. He'd made sure his aide had a sat phone as well in case he ran into any problems. The phone rang a few times before Damon finally answered.

"Sorley."

"Everley here. How's it going out there?"

"It's going okay, Sir. I've run into a couple of situations but I'm still on task."

"What kind of situations? How far are you?"

"Mostly locals looking for help, I would imagine. I didn't stop to find out. The last one was an attempted carjacking or robbery. I didn't stop for that one either. I'm just north of Philadelphia on the New Jersey Turnpike. I'm thinking I should be there in two, three hours tops, Sir."

"Call me before you go into New York City, Damon," Everley said. "I'll see if I can find out Tanner's exact location in the meantime. I'm pretty sure you don't want to spend the night roaming around what will undoubtedly be a horrific situation. I can't even imagine what it will be like there."

Recent event still fresh in his mind, Damon replied, "I can, Sir. It will be hell, pure and simple. After a full day of no power, no cars, no phones, and no information whatsoever from anyone in a position of power, I'm guessing it will resemble a war zone. But I'll find out when I get there. I'll call you in a couple of hours, General."

"Stay safe, Major," Everley said. "I mean that."

"That's at the top of my list of priorities right now, Sir."

Everley ended the call on his end. Laying the phone back down on his desk, he actually tried to imagine what New York City was like right then. Over eight and a half million people in a city that covered roughly three hundred square miles made it the highest population density of any city in the United States. The sheer volume of people, combined with the limited resources of the police and National Guard, if they had even been called out, was an impossible situation to fathom. When the water stopped flowing and the sewage treatment plants ceased to function, places like New York City would become literal cesspools of disease. Lawlessness would rule the streets, which would probably be taken over by the gangs that were already there. A city with strict gun control, most residents would have no way to defend themselves against thieves, rapists, and murderers, all of which would rise from the dark holes they usually hid in to walk boldly down the street — unhindered, unfettered, and uncontrolled. All the gun laws meant nothing to them. They didn't abide by the law.

Charles shuddered at the thought and felt a moment of remorse for sending Damon into that madness. But this wasn't about one major. It wasn't about him, either. It was about doing whatever they could to save the country they had sworn to protect and serve. The Republic was in danger, and it was their duty to do whatever was within their power to save it.

Chapter 21

The closer they got to the Dollar Tree, the more people they encountered. Their idea of staying across the street from the store to hopefully avoid the crowd there was not meant to be. Those attempting to gain access to the store filled the parking lot, the street, and the sidewalk across from it that Will and Amanda were trying to use to get around them. The crowd was loud and sounded angry. Apparently, this store was denying access to the people as well. Their approach did not go unnoticed as several men came from the street and met them on the sidewalk.

"Hey, buddy, did you guys find some supplies? Where'd you get them?" one man asked. He was talking to Will, but he was eyeing their packs.

Will stopped and addressed the man. "No, we haven't found any supplies. We had these with us already. We've been walking since early this morning. We're tired and we're just trying to get home. If you'll excuse us ..." Will took Amanda's hand and attempted to step around the man. The stranger stepped in front of him again.

"Well, what's in those packs you're carrying? Maybe we could do a trade or something."

Will shook his head as he replied, "Sorry, but we aren't looking to trade. We've still got a little way to go, and we'll need what we have to get there. Now please, let us pass."

A look passed between the man and his two companions. Suddenly, one of the men grabbed Amanda and the other two grabbed Will. Amanda screamed, and Will yelled, "Get off me! Let go of her!"

The men were trying to pull the backpacks from both of them. Amanda's hiking pack had a buckle that closed in the front to keep it stabilized and in the proper position for balance and comfort. The man who had grabbed her was trying to pull her pack from her, but the buckle kept that from happening. She struggled to free herself from his grasp, slapping at his head with both hands. When he stepped in front of her to try to open the buckle, she brought a knee up between his legs. He immediately released her, placing both hands over his crotch, and backed away howling in pain. Reaching behind her, Amanda felt for the bottom of her pack. Finding what she was after, she pulled out a collapsible hiking pole and started beating her attacker with it. She continued to scream, but it was a rage-filled sound, not scared.

"Get your hands off me, you piece of shit! Who do you think you are, grabbing me, trying to take my things? How dare you touch me!" About every fourth word was punctuated with her hitting him again with the compact pole. The would-be thief was on his knees alternating between protecting his head and shoulders and his groin area while crying out in anguish.

That altercation got the attention of everyone in the area, including the other two men who had grabbed Will. With their focus off of him, Will was able to free his right hand, reach into his coat pocket, and pull out the exposed blade. He stabbed the spokesman for the trio in the left forearm causing the man to release him and withdraw to yelp in pain. That only left the third man who, seeing his companions under attack, released Will and took a couple of steps backwards raising his hands in a submissive posture. Will held the knife in front of him watching the two men who had attacked him. Amanda continued her assault on her own attacker. Neither of his friends tried to stop her. Still keeping an eye on his own assailants, Will reached out a hand and tentatively touched Amanda's arm.

"Amanda ... it's okay ... you can stop now. I don't think he's going to mess with you anymore," Will said softly.

"You bet your *ass* —" she punctuated the last word with another rap across his shoulders, "he isn't. Dick! Get the hell away from me!"

Her attacker tried to stand and stumbled, slipping on the ice instead. He had multiple cuts on his head from Amanda's beating. Nothing life-threatening, but he would have one hell of a headache very soon. When she brandished her makeshift weapon at him as if to strike him again, he all but crawled away from her quickly on all fours, whimpering. When he reached his companions, they leaned down and helped him to his feet. Supporting their beaten friend, the three men backed away from Will and Amanda as quickly as they could on the frozen ground. When they were well out of reach, the spokesman called out.

"There wasn't no call for all that! We just wanted to know what you had in them packs!"

"What we have in our packs is none of your business," Will replied. "You might ought to think twice about attacking people. Just because you outnumber someone doesn't mean you have the advantage. Now step aside unless you want my friend here to continue the lessons." He inclined his head towards Amanda, who raised the folded hiking pole as if to punctuate his statement.

The attackers moved into the street clearing the sidewalk in front of Will and Amanda. Onlookers behind them got out of the way as well. As the two started down the sidewalk away from the store area, they were met with hostile looks and curious stares. Amanda kept her makeshift weapon out, as did Will his knife. They instinctively walked in a manner that let them keep their eyes on the crowd, even turning to walk backwards as they got past the store. Will didn't relax until they turned the corner onto 4th Avenue and the Dollar Tree was out of sight. He walked them past the first couple of houses and finally stopped in the middle of the road.

"How are you doing, Obi-Wan?" he asked playfully as he silently inspected her for damage. She seemed to be no worse for the wear outside of the wild look in her eye.

"That was just … just unreal. I've never been attacked before, have you?" He thought he detected a slight tremble in her voice as she spoke.

He shook his head and said, "No, that was a first for me, too. Unfortunately, it probably won't be the last. Please answer my question: are you okay?"

"I think so. Just scared and pissed off. Do you think that's going to happen a lot now?" she asked anxiously.

Again, it was on the tip of his tongue to tell her about the visions. He didn't think, he knew it was going to happen, more and more. But with what they had just been through, he wasn't sure how she would handle the knowledge of a psychic traveling companion on top of everything else. Hoping she would see it as an assumption on his part, he said, "I do, and probably pretty soon. People do crazy things when their lives are turned upside down. You see what the stores are like, and it hasn't even been twenty-four hours since everything went down. There are probably thousands of people living within a square mile of where my parents live. Definitely hundreds. All those people with no power, running out of food, it can't help but get ugly."

"I still don't understand why it got violent so fast," she replied. "I mean, surely people are not out of food already. I could probably last three or four days if I was stuck in my dorm room with the food I have there."

"Without a microwave? Or the single burner cooktop you probably have?"

Amanda considered what he'd said. "Yeah, I forgot about that. Most of what I have is add water and nuke for five minutes. So, if lots of other people had the same kind of foods that I have …"

"They're all looking for something that doesn't need electricity to be able to eat it now. If this goes on, in a week there won't be a saltine cracker or spoon of peanut butter anywhere. And that will suck, because I love peanut butter and crackers."

Amanda sighed. "Me, too. Well, now what?"

"We get to Mom and Dad. Follow me."

Will continued west on 4th Avenue. The houses in this area were built around 1990. They had decent sized lots and were not right on top of each other. They were walking down the street when Will heard the distinct sound of the motor. His eyes lit up as he said, "I hear something! Come on!" They picked up their pace as much as they could without slipping on the ice-covered road. As they got closer, they could tell it was more than one of whatever it was. Rounding a curve in the street, they came upon an unexpected sight.

Four riding lawnmowers were coming toward them single file, two with trailers. They slid a bit on the frozen surface, but they were definitely moving. Will's face lit up with a huge grin. He turned to Amanda. "This is great! This means some things made it through the pulse."

Will's glee was infectious. Amanda smiled back at him and said, "Awesome! Do you think I can find someone who'll let me use theirs to get to Rhinelander?"

Will laughed out loud at that. "I just had a mental picture of you on a riding mower going up Interstate 55. I don't think those tires are made for that kind of trip. You better stick with me for now."

Amanda sighed dramatically. "Fine, if I have to. How much further is it?"

"Just a few blocks. Hey, I think I know that guy." Will was pointing to the man in front of the mower line. As they drew closer, the gentleman's face sparked in recognition.

"Will! Oh, man, is it good to see you! Your parents are going to be so happy. They're worried sick about you. I was there just a little while ago. Your dad gave me the idea to see if my riding mower would work. I'm not sure about the newer ones, but these older models seem to have made it through this mess."

Will stretched a gloved hand out to him. "Hey, Jack. Glad to see or hear something running. Was Carly there?"

Jack nodded. "Yep, she's with them. We're headed to the Dollar Tree to see if there's anything we can pick up for cash."

Will scowled and said, "Don't bother. It's full of people and the doors are locked. Although from what we've seen this morning, that won't last long."

"What do you mean?"

Will went on. "We came down Stage Road. Walmart, Lowe's, Target, Wolfchase — they're covered with looters. I know for sure the mobs broke into Walmart and Lowe's. And Kroger up on Summer? Someone got shot when the front windows were taken out."

"Are you serious?" Jack said shocked. "Right next to the police station? Where were the cops?"

Will shrugged. "Honestly, I haven't seen one all morning. No police, sheriff, troopers, nothing. I guess they know they're outnumbered, or they're home trying to take care of their own families."

"Well, that completely sucks," Jack said. "I was hoping to get some more food, maybe some other stuff for *my* family. After talking to your dad this morning, looks like we're in for a rough ride. But, speaking of families, since the stores are a bust, you want a ride home?"

Will laughed. "I walked fifteen miles in snow, freezing rain, slipping on ice and now I get offered a ride when I'm like three, four blocks from home. Hell yeah!" He turned to Amanda. "Oh, shit, sorry. Amanda, this is Jack Duncan. He lives by my parents. Jack, this is Amanda Frye. We met on the road. She lives in Wisconsin and was on her way there when everything went down. I invited her to come home with me."

Amanda smiled and extended a hand toward Jack. "Please forgive my traveling companion's lack of manners. I'm sure he was raised better than that. I fully intend to ask his mother after I meet her. Very pleased to make your acquaintance, Jack."

Jack snorted with laughter. "Ha! Got yourself a feisty one there, Will. Pleased to meet you, too, Amanda. Well, hop in, you two. Take a load off and enjoy the scenery. We have a winter wonderland and it's cold as hell. Well, hell probably isn't cold, but you know what I mean."

Will and Amanda climbed in the trailer. Will sat down, stretched his legs out, closed his eyes and let out a long "Ahhhhhh." Amanda shrugged out of her pack, laid it beside him, and sat on it.

"You can say that again. By the way, this metal trailer is freezing. Isn't your butt getting cold?"

"My butt's been cold for the last several hours. In about five minutes, I'll be standing in front of a roaring fire at home. I can last that long."

Chapter 22

Carly's mind was spinning with information overload and unanswered questions. How could something like this happen? She knew how it happened, or at least what her dad thought of the situation, but how could the government have let them be put in this position? Why didn't they try to protect the power grid from something like this? If they couldn't, why didn't they let the people know it was a possibility? More important than any of that ... how was she going to get to her boys? Were they okay? The not knowing was driving her nuts — and making her very cranky.

"Carly? Did you hear what I said? Carly!" Lauri said loudly.

"What! No! What did you say?" she replied rudely.

Lauri put her hands on her hips. "Excuse me — I don't believe I raised you to talk to your mother that way."

Carly rolled her eyes. *What am I, twelve?* she thought. Sullenly, she said aloud, "Sorry. What did you say, Mom?"

"I said, what do you think about going ahead and bringing some bedding in here for us to sleep tonight? The fireplace basically heats this room. If we do it now while there's still daylight, we won't be rummaging around in the dark later."

"Yeah, that sounds like a plan. Where are they? I'll get them," Carly said, rising from the sofa.

"Sheet sets are in the linen closet, and pillows and blankets are in the closet in your old room. Come on, I'll show you." Lauri started down the hall and Carly followed.

When they walked into the room that Carly had grown up in, she stopped and stared as Lauri walked over to the closet door. Not that she hadn't seen them before but seeing the two twin beds that her sons used when they would spend the night there brought a flood of emotions to her. Sitting at the foot of the one closest to the door, she started crying again. Lauri turned at the sound.

"Why? Why did this have to happen today? Yesterday they would've been home. They'd be here with me, with us. I don't think I can make it through this, Mom, not without my boys. And I can't figure anyway we can get to them. I can't, I just can't do this without them. I can't think about anything but them, wondering if they're all right, crazy with not knowing. What am I gonna do?" Carly was sobbing uncontrollably, almost gasping for air. Lauri set the blankets and pillows on the other bed and went to her daughter. She put her arm around her and Carly laid her head on her mother's shoulder.

"I don't know why this happened today or any day. Crazy people do things sane people can't understand. I do know this though. We will get to Aaron and Cameron, and Elliott. We'll figure something out. That's a promise." The conviction in Lauri's tone was so strong that Carly raised her head and looked at her mother.

"How can you promise that, Mom? We have no way to get there. And don't say the riding mower, because that's ridiculous. We need a car or a truck that works. Do those things even exist anymore?" Her breathing was calming down with only slight hitches every couple of minutes as she tried to get control of herself.

Lauri stood, leaned over to kiss her daughter on top of her head, then walked over to retrieve the blankets and pillows. She carried them back to Carly, who stood as well, and took the load from her mother. Lauri calmly replied, "Because your dad won't rest until we're all together again. If there's a way to get there, he'll figure it out. Until then, we just have to trust Elliott to take care of the boys — and you know he will. If we can't have them with us, that's

173

where I'd want them to be. Take that bedding to the living room and go wash your face. I'll get the rest of what we need."

"Yes, ma'am," Carly said as she headed down the hall. Lauri closed her eyes and sent up a silent prayer.

Lord, please keep our boys safe while we're not with them, all four of them. Amen.

Joel was coming in from the garage when Lauri entered the living room with the sheets. She looked up at the sound of the door from the garage closing.

"What were you doing out there, dear?" she asked as she laid the sheets on top of the blankets Carly had set down earlier.

Slipping off his duck boots and sliding into his house shoes, Joel hung his coat on the doorknob and went to the fire to warm up. "I went ahead and shut the generator off and brought it in the garage. Carly's cooler has quite a few drinks in it — sodas, juice, that sort of thing — so we can use out of that for tonight. If I remember right, the forecast was gonna keep us pretty chilly over the next few days temperature wise, so we should be able to utilize coolers on the patio and in the garage to keep stuff cold, especially things you go into the refrigerator a lot for, like drinks. We should probably get the sandwich meat and cheese out tomorrow first thing and put it in a cooler outside. It will keep it colder there than in the fridge."

Lauri smiled at him. "Already done. I pulled it out when I got the roast together. The ice in the ice maker had apparently started melting before you turned the generator on, because it was a big block of ice when I checked on it. I pulled it out, put it in a cooler, and put the lunchmeat and cheeses in with it, along with the milk. Lucky for us our eggs *don't* come from the grocery store since we don't have to refrigerate them if we haven't washed them. I set the cooler by the patio door just a few minutes ago."

"That's my smart girl. Let me warm these old bones a minute and I'll put it out back with Carly's. Speaking of Carly, where is she?"

Lauri's smile disappeared. Lowering her voice, she all but whispered, "She's in the bathroom cleaning herself up. She had a little meltdown a few minutes ago. She's just beside herself about Aaron and Cameron not being here. I tried to reassure her that we would find a way to them but honestly, Joel, I'm right there with her. The not knowing about Will — where he is, if he's okay, if he's on his way home — I have to keep myself busy, so I don't dwell on it or we would be sitting next to each other sharing a crying jag. I truly believe our grandsons are in the best hands they could be in during something like this, and I'm a lot less worried about them than our son at the moment."

Joel wrapped his arms around his wife. The top of her head came to just below his chin as she returned his embrace. They stood like that for a moment comforting each other. He took a step back, looked down into her eyes, and said, "Our son will get home. I expect he'll be here before dark, if not sooner. For now, let's get that cooler on the patio and check your roast."

"Did someone say cooler?" Carly asked as she was coming into the room. "I'm pretty sure there's still some beer out there, if anyone wants to join me."

"I will," Joel replied. "It may be the last beer we see for a while." He grabbed his coat and boots and went to the sliding door that led out to the patio. Lauri followed with potholders. Joel set their cooler beside Carly's, then reached inside hers and pulled two beers out. He held one toward Lauri, who shook her head. Passing the beer bottles to Carly at the door, he went to the grill and opened the lid.

The aroma was wonderful. Lauri took the cover off the Dutch oven and smiled.

"I do believe it's done. I'll take it inside and make sure, but I think you can go ahead and turn the grill off."

"Oh my God, Mom, that smells amazing! Now I'm starving!" Carly exclaimed.

"Well, it needs to rest for a few minutes, but I think supper is ready. My goodness, it's getting colder out here. Let's get this inside before it cools off."

The three of them walked in and stamped the snow from their shoes onto the towel Lauri had left by the door in an attempt to keep the floors as dry as possible. Joel had carried in the heavy cast-iron cooking pot and was just about to set it on the table when they heard a key in the front door lock. No one said a word as the door opened and Will stepped through with a woman they didn't know. Lauri's sharp intake of breath was the first sound anyone made. Will grinned, threw up his hands, and said, "Surprise! Merry Christmas!"

Carly, Joel, and Lauri all but ran to the front door. Lauri got there first and hugged her son fiercely. "Thank you, Lord, for getting our boy home. Oh, honey, you made it, you're here! We've been so worried! Are you all right? Are you hungry? Come in, both of you. Hi, I'm Lauri, Will's mother."

Will laughed. "Hi, Mom. If you'd let me get a word in edge wise I'd show the lady I have some manners. Amanda, this is my mom, Lauri; my dad, Joel; and my sister, Carly. Guys, this is Amanda Frye. We met on the road, and I'll tell you the rest of it after I get in front of the fire and get a hot cup of coffee in my hand, although that beer Carly is holding looks pretty good, too."

Amanda closed the door behind her and stood watching the reunion between Will and his family. Once they had welcomed their son and brother home, they pulled her into their embrace as well. Carly held her for a moment and whispered in her ear, "Thank you for helping my brother get home."

Amanda whispered back, "We helped each other."

Will and Amanda were pulled into the living room and relieved of their packs and coats. They stood side-by-side in front of the fire, warming first their hands and front and then their backs. Lauri asked Amanda how she took her coffee.

"Heavy on the Baileys if you have it. It's been that kind of day, you know?"

Carly laughed as she headed for the kitchen. "Oh, I like her already. I'll have what she's having. The beer can wait."

The next hour was spent recounting each other's day, though Will and Amanda's was much more eventful. When Will described the blast he'd seen, Joel nodded solemnly. "Yep, sounds like my theory is correct. If it lit the sky like that, we're definitely gonna be in the worst-case scenario."

"Which is?" Amanda asked.

"The end of the world as we knew it, at least for the next few years," Joel replied.

Amanda's jaw dropped. "Years? Did you say years? Why years? Oh my God, I'm never getting home!"

Joel explained about the grid and transformers and sub-stations. When he found out home for her was Rhinelander, they spent a few minutes talking about that before Will turned to Carly. He had noticed the boys weren't there.

"Aaron? Cam?"

Her bottom lip started to tremble. Lauri reached for her hand and looked at Will. "They're safe. They're with Elliott."

Picking up on the tension, Will replied, "Hell yeah they're safe if they're with him. They're probably safer than we are. At least Elliott can defend himself and his place.

177

After what we ran into on the road, we're going to wish we had some of his guns."

Joel turned sharply to his son. "What happened out there?"

Will told them about the encounters on the highway, how some people had turned desperate quickly. Then he told them about the mobs on Stage Road. He told them about the attempted muggings — the first they were able to talk their way out of, the second they fought their attackers off. He looked at Amanda as he retold the story, while his family sat staring at them in shock.

"Amanda here turned out to be an accurate kicker," he said with a smile.

Amanda shrugged and replied, "Most guys are easily distracted by a well-placed knee to the junk."

"Dear God, Will. You were mugged in broad daylight, right up the street from here?" Lauri asked in a fear-tinged tone.

"Yeah, Mom. It's going to shit pretty quick out there. With all the people we saw on the streets, I'd bet the stores will be empty of any food in twenty-four hours or less. After that, it's probably going to get even uglier."

When he relayed the story of the hold-up and the shooting at Kroger, Carly interrupted. "Did you say Lauren? The girl who got shot ... her name was Lauren?"

"I think so. Yeah, I'm pretty sure that's what I heard."

Lauri looked at Carly. "What is it, honey? Did you know her?"

Carly replied, "She checked me out Saturday. She was young, like barely older than Aaron. Why would they do that? Break into the store, shoot at people, kill a young girl like that?"

"Because when people are scared they do crazy things, Carly," Joel answered. "Lots of others would have figured out when the cars and electronics wouldn't work this wasn't an ordinary power outage, even if they didn't know exactly what it really was. The strongest instinct in human nature is to survive. Survival means food, water, shelter, and protection. I'm sure those people would have been more than willing to pay for the food they looted, but unless they had cash, they wouldn't have been able to buy it, so they took it. In a few days, the cash won't be accepted anymore, once folks figure out it isn't worth anything now. You say all the stores you saw were being looted, Will?"

"Yep. They hadn't broken into Dollar Tree yet, but my guess is they have by now. I don't think our cash will do any good, Dad. Everything close will be cleaned out tonight, or tomorrow morning at the latest."

"That's fine. We aren't going to use our cash for food anyway. We need something else, much more important," Joel said.

"What's that?" Will asked his father.

Joel replied resolutely, "Guns."

Chapter 23

"Nana is never going to let you give up your bed, Pap," Aaron said as they talked about how to make room for four more people in the three-bedroom home. The twin beds the boys slept in were actually bunk beds that hadn't been stacked for years. Elliott had them put the bunks back together, leaving half of the room open for a pallet on the floor, as Elliott called it.

"I'm not sleeping on those wooden things, Pap," Cameron had commented at Elliott's phrase. "Just put me a sleeping bag on the floor or something."

Elliott laughed at his younger grandson. "Not a wood pallet, like for shipping things. A bed of blankets on the floor is called a pallet, too. And, yes, you being the youngest, you'll probably end up there so your Uncle Will can have one of the beds." He turned to Aaron. "As for your grandmother, she's not the only one who can be stubborn. There's no sense in me having that big bed all to myself. I can sleep in my recliner in the living room. Lord knows I've done that more than once. Then your mother can have the other bedroom." Elliott had worked it all out in his head earlier and was sure they could all fit in the house — if not comfortably, at least securely.

His biggest concern was how they would get out there with no modern vehicles running. They couldn't walk it. There was no way Joel or Lauri were in shape for something like that, any more than he was. He could go after them on his tractor. He had a ball hitch on it and a large trailer that would haul them and a lot of their stuff. The problem with that idea was they would all be exposed. If someone wanted to steal whatever they happened to have with them, the tractor wasn't built for speed and they could easily be overtaken, lose everything, and possibly get someone hurt. He was still considering it, but for now he felt like they should just stay put and hope Joel came up with a remedy.

He went to the kitchen to start supper. He called out, "Boys! Get in here! I'm fixin' to teach you how to cook fried pork chops and taters!"

After they ate and cleaned up the kitchen, Elliott heated water for hot chocolate for the boys. He had kept a pot of coffee on the back of the wood stove all day. It was strong, but he liked it that way. They sat in the living room enjoying their hot drinks and the warmth from the stove, each apparently lost in his own thoughts. Kerosene lamps that were sitting on tables close by cast a warm glow over the room. The lack of ambient noise caused by appliances that used electricity seemed very obvious. The silence was thick, like a fog inside the house.

"Wow, it's really quiet now," Cameron said softly from the couch, as if the sound of his voice could somehow disturb the stillness.

Elliott nodded. "Yep, you don't realize how much noise is around you all the time until it isn't. I'm betting a lot of folks are going to have trouble sleeping for a while, especially the ones who left a TV on all night in their room."

"No TV for me, but I did have the radio on my alarm clock on when I went to sleep. Definitely going to miss that," Aaron said.

Cameron sat up and exclaimed, "No more alarm clocks! No more school! Holy sh— um, cow ... no more school!"

"Oh, there'll be school, just a different kind," Elliott commented. "You'll be going to the school of 'Your Life Without Electricity.' There will be classes in 'How to Hunt, Grow, and Preserve Food if You Don't Want to Starve',

'How to Fix Your Own Leaky Roof', and 'How to Patch Holes in Your Clothes Because Nobody Is Making Them Anymore' for starters. The stuff they don't teach you in school is everything you're going to need to know now."

"Yeah, school was definitely not preparing us for this life," Aaron added. "In fact, I said something to that effect to Mom when she told us we were coming out this week, that I always learn things from you and Nana and Pops that I don't get in school. I already learned a bunch of cool stuff from you today."

Elliott grinned at his oldest grandson. "That's good, son, because we're just getting started. Tomorrow I'm gonna teach you guys how to milk a goat and clean out her stall."

"How come you never taught us how to milk her before? She's been here a while and we've been here lots of times." Cameron scrunched up his face when he said, "And that stall cleaning sounds gross. It's got goat poop in it, doesn't it? I'll probably hurl."

Aaron laughed at hearing his grandfather cackling as he replied, "Well, if you hurl, Cam, you'll have to clean that up, too, just so you know. Until your mom and grandmother get here, we're bachelors. We gotta take care of ourselves." Elliott paused for a moment, then went on. "And the reason I never taught you the milking before was … well … the only thing that comes to mind is that I didn't think it was something you were gonna need to know to get through life. I sure never expected anything like this to happen. Now that it has, all our priorities are changed. Before, we were just going along taking everything for granted: electricity, grocery stores, gas stations, that kind of stuff. Now, everything we do is going to be about our survival, or it should be. No time to waste on stupid reality shows or video games, which are gone for who knows how long. We'll be working all day on living and will probably be so tired at night we pass out asleep. But, in case you have a hard time falling asleep, I have some good books you can read. Outside of regular checkers and Chinese checkers, or card games, that's the closest thing to leisure time we'll probably see."

"Nice. What kind of books, Pap?" Aaron asked. "I'm always up for a good read."

"Well, I've got a bunch of Louis L'Amour westerns and quite a few prepper fiction books."

Cameron cocked his head to the side. "Prepper fiction? What's that about?"

Elliott replied solemnly, "Basically, it's about what our lives will be like now. I guess all that prepper fiction is turning into non-fiction as we speak."

"I think I'll start there," Aaron said. "Sounds like that may be our new school books."

"It very well may be, Aaron. They're on the book shelf behind you." Elliott pointed to a fully loaded built-in bookcase on the wall.

Aaron walked over and started skimming over the books there. "Well, I can't say I recognize any of these authors."

"That's because most of them are what is called indie authors. They publish their own books online without a publisher. Doesn't make them any less of a good read though," Elliott said. "And they usually don't cost as much. Read a few and let me know if you like them."

Aaron pulled out a book called *Good Fences* by an author named Boyd Craven and held it up. "How about this one, Pap? Any good?"

Elliott smiled and nodded. "Yep, that's a real good one and very fitting for our situation. I think you'll like it."

"What about me, Pap? Any suggestions?" Cameron asked.

Elliott walked over to the bookshelf and looked through the offerings. He pulled out a book and handed it to his younger grandson. "*One Second After*. It's about an EMP also. It's one of the first ones I ever read. This one isn't exactly prepper fiction. The folks in this story weren't prepared in any way for what happened. But it does tell how they adapted to the world they were left with, which is exactly what we're going to have to do."

Both boys settled down on the couch with their reading material. Elliott went back to his recliner and sipped his day-old coffee while watching the fire dance in the glass door of the wood-burning stove. His thoughts went again to Carly and the rest of the family. Not living in town and having no way or desire to get there, he had no idea what it was like where they were. He was sure it wasn't a good situation — he just didn't know how bad it was by then. He sent up a silent prayer that they were all together, safe and warm, and working out a way to get there.

The sun, which had finally peeked out right at dusk, had dropped below the horizon leaving a dark, silent world in its wake. Even though he lived in the country, there was a yard light that came on automatically at night bathing the top of the driveway, the carport, and part of the porch in light each evening. Glancing out the window and seeing nothing but blackness was a bit unnerving. He got up and checked that the front door was locked and bolted. The guns they had cleaned earlier were lying on his grandmother's old table in the kitchen. He picked up a small pistol, stuck it in his pants pocket, then checked the back door as he had the front. Satisfied they were as secure as they could be, he went back to the living room. He walked to the bookshelf and picked out a book for himself. He sat back down, took a sip of his coffee, and opened the book.

Cameron looked up from his tome. "What are you reading, Pap?"

Elliott held his book up. "*The Last Layover*. First book in one of my favorite series of prepper books, and it's based here in Tennessee."

"Sweet. I may read that one next," Cameron said as he went back to his own.

The sound of footsteps on the back porch had Elliott jumping out of his chair and reaching into his pocket for the pistol he had just placed there. At their grandfather's sudden movement, both boys sat up and looked at him, then toward the kitchen.

"What is it, Pap? You think maybe it's Roger again?" Aaron asked anxiously.

Elliott shook his head, speaking softly. "No, Roger wouldn't make that trip again; damn sure not at night." He pulled the pistol out of his pocket as he spoke.

Cameron's eyes grew wide. "Whoa! Are you gonna shoot 'em? Whoever's out there?"

"Shh!" Elliott hissed at Cameron. "I ain't planning to shoot anybody, but I wasn't expecting any company either. You boys stay in here." Elliott started toward the back door. The knock that came next made him jump.

Cameron whispered loudly, "They knocked. Robbers wouldn't knock, would they?"

Elliott continued on without acknowledging Cameron's remark. The back door was solid and didn't have a peep hole. Just as he was about to call out asking who it was, there was another knock and a voice that said, "Dad? Are you home?"

Elliott stopped dead in his tracks. He knew that voice. He hurried over to the door and unlocked it. Throwing it open, he found his son shivering in the dark. The shock was quickly replaced with joy. "Ethan! Sweet Jesus!"

Ethan smiled and said, "Hi, Dad. Can I come in? Pretty well frozen here."

Elliott reached for his only child. "Yes! Yes, come in!" He pulled Ethan inside the door, closed it behind him, and reset the locks. They stood there looking at each other awkwardly for a moment. Elliott extended his hand toward his son, who took it, then pulled his father into his embrace. Elliott hugged Ethan fiercely, with joyful tears coursing down his face. They stood in the kitchen, father and son, holding onto each other for all they were worth. The world for both of them stood still in that moment. They were unaware of the two young men standing in the doorway between the living room and kitchen watching the scene in awe. Finally, the two men heard a voice that shattered the magic of the moment.

"What the hell are you doing here?"

Elliott and Ethan pulled away from each other. They both looked to where the boys stood. Ethan felt like he was looking into a time travel mirror. "Aaron? Cameron? Oh my god! You're here!" He started toward them, but Aaron stepped in front of his younger brother.

"I asked you a question. What the hell are you doing here?"

Cameron peered around his older brother. "Dad? Is it really you?"

Aaron turned on him. "Don't call him that! Dads don't run out on their kids, not caring if they live or die. Dads don't pretend their kids never existed. He's not a dad!"

Cameron recoiled at his brother's verbal assault. Elliott went to his grandsons. He laid a wrinkled hand on Aaron's arm. "Can we just sit down and talk, son? Yes, he has a lot of explaining to do. You're right to be wary. I am, too. But with what's happened, we might need each other to get through this. Can you hear him out? For me?"

The daggers Aaron was shooting at his father softened when he looked down at his grandfather. He nodded slowly, saying, "Fine. I'll listen to what he has to say for

186

you, Pap. I just won't believe any of it." He looked back up at Ethan defiantly.

Elliott patted his arm. "Thank you, Aaron. Now, let's sit down and talk in the kitchen." He turned back to Ethan. "Are you hungry? Want some coffee?" Ethan was still staring at his sons.

"I can't believe you're here. I had no idea … I mean, I was on my way here to surprise Dad for Christmas, and I'm the one who's surprised. This is just so great."

Aaron snorted. "Great? Did you miss the fact that our world is turned upside down? What's great about that?"

Despite his oldest son's belligerent tone, Ethan couldn't stop smiling. "That you and Cameron are here. That in the middle of all this shit, I finally get to see you both. It was just meant to be."

Aaron rolled his eyes. "Jesus, you sound like a sappy soap opera. Why would it be meant to be anything?"

Ethan's smile disappeared. His face was filled with sorrow and regret. "I've been a terrible father, a horrible son. I can't undo that. All I can do is try to get to know you now. Hopefully you can find it in your heart to forgive me."

"Forgive you? Why would you ever think we would forgive you?"

Ethan looked down at the floor then back into the mirror reflection of his eyes and said, "Because I'm dying."

Chapter 24

The Chairman had risen early, despite the long-lasting celebration he had hosted the night before. He reveled in the celebrity showered on him by his people. He puffed out his chest with pride at the praise heaped on him by the attendees. The only dark spot of the night had been the call from the president of the United Nations. He had no doubt that there would political repercussions from that body. He didn't care. Their sanctions meant nothing to him. He had allies who could see his vision of a crippled United States and were willing to support his actions and provide to his country what the United Nations and the United States had tried to deny them. Their support may have been in secret that day, but the days after were going to be a different story.

He had scheduled a meeting first thing in the morning with his top-ranking military leaders to determine how they would progress now that the attack had been successful. He sat at the head of a long, polished table. All the seats were filled on either side with military personnel in various states of wakefulness. Apparently, some of his underlings had celebrated a bit too much from the pained looks on their faces. That was their fault. He didn't force them to drink too much. There was no seat at the other end of the table. No one was in a position to equal his. Not even close. He addressed the group.

"Good morning, comrades. I trust you slept well after our glorious victory and subsequent celebration. Today, the eyes of the world are on us and our country. They are in awe of what we have done; what we have accomplished. No one thought the United States could be brought to this level. No one believed it could happen so quickly and cleanly. No loss of a single Korean life. No guns fired. And yet, we sit here victors in a battle fought thousands of miles away with the push of a button. A new day has dawned for North Korea. We will be revered as a force to not be taken lightly."

The men around the table nodded their heads in agreement. Timid smiles crossed the faces of a number of the attendees. The Chairman went on.

"In the coming days and weeks, we will formulate our plans to continue with the next phase of our attack. We will monitor closely the deterioration of the condition of the people. As they must adapt or die in this new reality, many will not be strong enough or brave enough to fight for their lives. They will die or be killed for the food in their homes and then soon, the clothes on their backs. When they have warred among themselves long enough, we will simply step in and take control. Are there any questions?"

A general tentatively raised his hand. The Chairman acknowledged him with an inclination of his head. "Excellency, what about their allies? Won't other countries that are loyal to the Americans come to their aid? Is there a chance they may attack us in retaliation?"

The Chairman snorted in disgust. "We have shown the world what we are willing to do to end oppression heaped on our country by pompous arrogant nations who have no respect for us or our way of life. No one would dare to attack us now."

At the far end of the table, one of the admirals leaned over to the man next to him and whispered, "Let us hope not, but I fear this is just the beginning of a battle we are destined to lose."

Excerpt from Book 3 in the Perilous Miles Series, Another 20 Miles

Chapter 1

Damon had been on the road for most of the day. He was stiff from sitting in the same position for so long, and his leg was aching from not being used. The sun setting behind him told him the day was coming to an end. He was still at least an hour from New York City. There was no way he was going in there alone at night. He needed to find a place to hunker down for the night.

He stopped again to consult his maps, both civilian and military. He took the opportunity to get out to stretch his legs and relieve himself. He had stopped just south of another residential area, Milltown, New Jersey. He could see signs up ahead for The Home Depot and Target in the waning remnants of daylight. That was definitely not an area where he could secure his vehicle, much less himself. He got back in the Humvee, locked the doors out of habit, pulled out a tactical flashlight, and consulted the map of bases and armories. His ride was a bit obvious, both because it was a military vehicle, and because it actually ran. He needed a place he could blend in.

He found a National Guard armory not far from his current location. It would take him off his preferred route, but he felt that the loss of travel time would be made up for in what he hoped would be a more secure location than out on the open road. The ramp off the turnpike to Highway 18, also known as Memorial Parkway, was just about a mile ahead. The area wasn't ideal. There were a lot of houses and apartments between him and the armory. There was a service road that provided access to the Raritan River he could use for a bit, but there just wasn't a route available that wouldn't have him driving through some heavy residential areas on the way. He just didn't have many options at that point. The closer he got to New York City, the more densely populated the area would become.

A fist hitting the driver's side window made Damon jump in surprise. He instinctively reached for his sidearm. Turning his head, he saw a man standing beside the vehicle trying to open the door. Finding it locked, the man beat his fist against the window again.

"Hey! Where'd you get the Hummer? How come yours runs and nobody else's does? Are you with the government? What's going on? Open the door!" The man rattled off question after question, punctuating each one with another fist to the window. Damon pulled his pistol up into view. The stranger took a couple of steps back but continued to stare at Damon with hate-filled eyes. Damon reached down and turned the ignition, firing up the Humvee. The man's eyes grew wide as he realized Damon was getting ready to leave. He took a step forward again, shouting, "Why aren't you helping us? Where is the government or the Red Cross? We're going to run out of food in just a couple of days! I've got three kids and no way to feed them! We need help!"

Damon looked at the man and replied sadly through the closed window, "I'm not here to help you. I don't know when or if help is coming. You need to go home and lock your doors. I'm sorry, I have to go. Good luck — you're going to need it. We all are." With that, Damon put the vehicle in gear and quickly pulled away. He could see the man in his rear-view mirror running behind him, slipping on the roads that were iced over with no traffic to melt it, shaking his fist and yelling something Damon could no longer hear. He wasn't lying when he told the man he was sorry — Damon felt genuine compassion for his plight. Damon was glad he hadn't married or had kids. He couldn't even fathom not being able to feed them in a place that seemed to have always been teeming with food. Fast food joints on every corner; restaurants for miles; even gas stations served hot food, so to speak. To think that in the amount of time it took to snap one's fingers it was all gone was more than he could process. He looked over at the snacks he had brought. He didn't know how long they would last. Hopefully long enough to get him to his destination. After that, he had no clue. He was no more prepared for a life without electricity than most of the other people in the country.

He continued on until he reached the exit for Memorial Parkway. As with all toll roads, there was one last booth before the end. Just like the others he had passed, the arms were broken, leaving Damon again to wonder who had come through in a working vehicle to do the damage. He hoped it was U.S. military. Any alternative he could imagine was not comforting.

The interchange was massive with more than a dozen lanes coming together. He couldn't help but think what a nightmare rush hour traffic was like here. There were quite a few abandoned cars in both directions but no people he could see. As it had been at least twelve hours since the blast, he was pretty certain anyone who had been driving through there had sought shelter before the sun went down. If he recalled correctly, the weather forecast had called for lows in the low teens along the Eastern seaboard north of D.C. for the next few days. Without shelter, proper clothing, or the right gear, people couldn't live through that. Considering most of the city populations heated their homes with electric heat, he knew many Americans would likely die of exposure, even if they were in their homes. At some point, without heat on the inside, it would come close to the temperature of the outside.

Damon was able to weave around the dead cars and trucks and made his entrance onto Memorial Parkway. It appeared most if not all of the residents in the area were inside their homes. He saw no one outside, thankfully. He progressed well to his next exit that would take him to Johnson Drive. Johnson Drive would become Hamilton Street, which was where the armory was located. He just had to get through about three miles of a heavily residential area first.

He had expected to see evidence of looting at grocery and convenience stores. He didn't expect to see restaurants with their doors kicked in. But then, why shouldn't he have? Restaurants were places with food, and usually a lot of it in industrial-sized cans or crates. Every one that he passed appeared to have been vandalized and stripped. *And this is just the first day,* he thought. *What will it be like in a week, when all the food is gone?*

There were a few places where people were congregated outside around barrels with their contents burning. The flames lit up the area around them showing the fear and uncertainty on their faces. At the sound of the Humvee, heads turned toward the street; a few of them even took steps toward him. Damon didn't slow down. In fact, if it looked like someone was heading his direction he sped up.

He was making his way down the street at a decent rate of speed until he reached the parking lot for a strip mall with a dollar store and a number of small restaurants. The lot was a decent size spanning Hamilton from one street to the next. And it had a lot of people in it. Damon could see from the kerosene lanterns and flashlights held by some of the people there that every storefront in the building had been broken in. At the sound of his approach, every flashlight beam was trained on the road in front of him, then his vehicle. Many of the onlookers hurried toward the sound. He tried to speed up again. He wasn't quick enough. At least half a dozen men stepped out and stretched across the two-lane street. He considered taking the sidewalk to his left, but his moment of hesitation gave the men time to block that as well. Damon stopped about a hundred feet from them, engine idling. He had a decision to make — and this one would probably cost someone their life.

When he didn't exit the vehicle, one of the men in the street raised a shotgun and leveled it at Damon's head. He called out, "You need to just come on out of that car, buddy. We don't want to hurt you. We just want that ride and anything in it."

Damon had both pistols in his lap. He knew there was no danger of the shotgun pellets piercing the glass — he just didn't know what other weapons they might have. He knew New Jersey had some of the strictest gun laws in the country. He also knew that not everyone who lived there agreed with having their Second Amendment rights violated. There would most definitely be guns about which the local and state authorities were in the dark.

When Damon didn't comply, the man yelled louder. "I said for you to get out of that Hummer! You hard of hearing? Don't make me shoot you!"

Damon picked up his Sig and held it up for the man to see. He rolled the window down ever so slightly and said, "I can't do that. I have orders. I'm on official military business. I'm going to need you men to clear the road. Don't make me run you down."

The man answered with a fake laugh. "Oh! Oh, I see — official military business. Real nice coincidence that your official military vehicle just happens to still be running when no one else's does. Why is that? And where's the rest of the military, or the National Guard ... hell anybody with some food and water would be great! I bet you have food and water in there with you though, huh? That's how this works — the government takes care of themselves and screw everybody else! You think we're stupid? You think we don't know this isn't going to get fixed overnight? We know! We figured it out. How are we supposed to feed our kids next week when there's no food now?"

The crowd grew louder at the man's comments, voicing their support for him and his companions in the middle of the street. Damon didn't blame them. He knew there were probably millions of people in the country who were thinking the same thing. He wished he had answers for them. He didn't. That was way above his pay grade. The crowd seemed to be moving toward the street to join the men blocking his way. Damon knew he had to move before they got there, or this would end bloody.

He revved the engine then put the gear shift in drive. He started forward slowly as he raised his head up to the small opening in the door window. "I don't know much more than you, sir. I can't help you. I have to go now. Either move or I will be forced to drive over you." He let the Humvee roll toward the line of men. He could see by the looks on their faces they didn't think he would hit them. He could also see the small bit of doubt that he might. They seemed to be inching away from their spokesman who was holding his ground, shotgun still pointed at Damon.

"You aren't leaving with that truck! Stop or I'll shoot!" When Damon didn't stop, the man fired at the windshield. Damon instinctively ducked even though the pellets from what was obviously bird shot did little more than ping off the glass. The man racked the gun to chamber a new round as Damon increased his speed. Seeing their companion's shot had no effect on the Humvee, his compatriots ran for the sidewalks on either side. The shooter seemed to be committed to holding his ground until Damon was about five feet away. At the last minute, he too dove for the sidewalk. Unfortunately, he wasn't quite quick enough. The grill over the front caught him in the side and pitched him up into the crowd gathered there. Damon didn't stop to check on him. He kept going until the crowd was no longer visible in his rear-view mirror. He had a slight tremor in his hands, undoubtedly from the adrenaline rush, but he knew he had had no choice but to do what he did. His task had to be completed. The fate of the country could very well depend on it.

He kept his speed up through the rest of the residential areas. The few people who were out looked up at the sound of the engine but thought better of approaching at the speed at which he was traveling. He arrived at the armory a few minutes later. There was no one manning the gate. He drove through and straight to the back of the building. He was hoping at least someone would be there to lend fire support if he needed it, but the place looked deserted. He was just about to rethink the choice when a flashlight lit up the cab of the Humvee and a voice called out, "I hope you didn't steal that ride, buddy. Let's see some ID."

Damon smiled. He might be okay after all.

Acknowledgments

Hello friends. I'm so glad to be able to bring you the next installment in the Perilous Miles series. As you have seen, many in this scenario have been portrayed as unprepared, for the most part, for what their lives will become now. I believe this is a very realistic portrayal of what society would be like if something like this happened. While I don't think people are stupid (as seen by the looters who quickly realized this wasn't just ice on the lines), they still haven't grasped that the food they are gathering won't last as long as the power outage will. It should be interesting to see the transformations from everyday Joe, to looter/scavenger of stores, to getting food wherever they can, regardless of who they have to go through to get it. What would you do to feed your kids if the stores were empty?

I really think I missed self-publishing. I missed the control I had over the entire process. I definitely missed working with my people. Jim never ceases to amaze me when I give him my ideas and some samples. The photo we used for to start working on the cover of this book looks very different from what he presented me as a final product. I love it. He keeps our place going while I write. We were without water for six days after that serious cold snap in January. He crawled around in the mud and muck every day until he got it back on. He is my biggest fan, and I couldn't do this without him and his support. Thank you, Baby.

My aunt, Carol, has had some health issues of late but she always makes time to edit my books. She finds things I didn't see after reading through multiple times. She spends hours researching to make sure what she sends me is correct – at least in someone's opinion. If you need a proofreader/editor, I can hook you up with her. Thank you, sweet aunt. Take care of you.

I can't say enough about my beta readers. These guys and gals find things that my aunt and I don't, even after the multiple read throughs. You just can't have enough eyes on something like this. They are voracious readers and loyal beyond words. Thank you, ART members. You help me put out the best product I can.

To all the loyal followers of my books, thank you for the kind words and messages. I never dreamed it would turn out like this when I wrote that first book. You honor and humble me. I hope I can continue to write stories that keep you wanting more.

Last, and most important, I give the glory to God that He blessed me with this gift to tell stories people want to read. I placed my life in His hands and all I have is because of Him. Thank you, Lord, for the many blessings you bestow upon me every day.

Book 3 in the Perilous Miles series, Another 20 Miles, will be available by summer. Stay tuned!

Find P.A. Glaspy on the web!

http://paglaspy.com/ – the website, always updating, so keep coming back for more info. Want to stay up to date on all our latest news? Join our mailing list for updates, giveaways, and events! You'll find a spot to sign up on the right side of the website. We don't spam, ever.

https://www.facebook.com/paglaspy/ – Facebook Fan Page

https://twitter.com/paglaspy – Follow on Twitter

https://www.amazon.com/P.A.-Glaspy/e/B01H131TOE/ref=sr_tc_2_0?qid=1475525227&sr=8-2-ent – Amazon Author Page

https://www.goodreads.com/author/show/15338867.P_A_GLASPY – Goodreads Author Page

https://www.bookbub.com/authors/p-a-glaspy – BookBub Author Page